SINFONIA:

FIRST NOTES ON THE
LUTE

I0620960

A Vampire Chronicle
Book One

DAVID W. LANDRUM

Sinfonia: First Notes on the Lute
Copyright © 2016 by David W. Landrum

Cover Art
Mac Hernandez
Editor-in-Chief
Kristi King-Morgan
Formatting
Niki Browning

Printed in the United States of America

First Printing, 2016

ISBN 13: 978-0692701065
ISBN 10: 0692701060

Dreaming Big Publications

www.dreamingbigpublications.com

I

Thunderous applause greeted Nelleke Reitsma as she walked out on stage carrying her lute. Her brown hair shook as she walked. She carried her lute in one hand and smiled as the enthusiastic audience applauding her. She remembered how her mother would chide her for looking so stern. A serious, no-nonsense attitude had always been a part of her personality when she was mortal, but that was long ago. Tonight she smiled for the large crowd that came out to see her perform.

The bright stage lights burned her brown eyes and she reflected, just briefly, how different it was from the first time she had played her lute by candlelight. Nelleke Reitsma, not tall but slender, with dark brown hair, deep-set eyes, and a wide, pretty smile knew how to use her good looks to advantage when she performed, always carefully making herself over to accentuate her eyes and mouth and dressing in a manner different from most women who played guitar or lute. She cut a striking, lovely figure as she took her place on the stage.

A capacity crowd filled the concert hall. The concert had sold out in one day. Nelleke ranked as one of the most popular lutenists and guitarists in the world, but the announcement that for this recital she would play a hitherto unknown suite by the English musician John Bull had packed the place to capacity. She knew the crowd contained music critics and historians and that articles on the pieces she would play would be in journals and on webpages within an hour of the closing song. She had carefully kept the pieces all these years so she could present them at the proper time, which was now.

She sat down in the chair on the stage, tossed back her brown hair (which she wore long and loose), crossed her legs, spread a black cloth across her thighs so the lute would not slide off her black nylons. She smiled into the pelting waves of applause. Nelleke performed in short skirts almost always now. It had been a good publicity move and added to the image she had constructed of herself as the edgy, risqué lady of the classical musical world. Once more, she thought of the contrast. It had been easier in the old days with long skirts, but it had been so stiflingly hot. Though the way she dressed now called for caution, she felt cooler and more comfortable. She waited for the audience to quiet down. The sound of applause fell from the roar of a waterfall to the rush of a cascade to a smattering like rainfall and then to silence. When the audience quieted completely, she spoke.

"Thank you, ladies and gentlemen, so much. I'm honored to be able to play here in Carnegie Hall and I am even more honored to perform, this night, a group of hither-to unknown compositions by one of Renaissance England's greatest composers. It's customary to start a concert with a fast, rousing piece to set the mood, but since I know many of you have come to hear the suite by John Bull, I'm going to play that first. Let me say just a couple of words about it."

She talked about how she had discovered the piece of music in a drawer at an English courthouse. The people had given it to her even when she assured them it was valuable and a historical discovery of some significance. She had hired a lawyer and they had signed a release giving the musical score to her. They said they wanted it in the hands of a capable musician who would cherish it and could perform it all over the world. Bull had lived in their village, they said, and they venerated him. They wanted anything he had composed there played on a global scale and thus were happy to give control of the music to her.

Indeed, John Bull had written the lute suite and the occasional pieces she would play tonight. He had composed them in the village she mentioned in her introduction. The untruth in her story was that he had written them specifically for her and given them to her in exchange for her sexual favors.

Nelleke let her mind return to the present. Concentration was vital to a performing musician. You could not let your mind drift from the piece you were playing. Silence fell in the concert hall as the audience anticipated a composition new to them, and to the music world, but one she had played and practiced for hundreds of years. She launched into the notes she knew so well and perform with the dynamic they deserved.

When she had finished and the audience applauded wildly, Nelleke smiled inwardly. John Bull, she reflected, would feel quite a bit of chagrin if he could know she had kept his composition hidden from 1611 to 2012.

II

Nelleke Reitsma's journey had begun in 1574, when she was eighteen years old and the City of Utrecht garrisoned some of its troops in the town of Ijsselstein during the religious wars. Garrisons moved into the city and camped around the river. Soldiers prowled in groups, making the populace wary. People warned her not to go out alone, but one night she stayed for prayers with the nuns in the church where she took music lessons. Carrying her lute, she made her way back home in the early hours of darkness down a quiet back street where she thought she would not encounter anyone.

She turned the corner and felt a sudden mighty blow to the left side of her head. She fell to the ground, dazed. Nelleke lay there in the soft mud of the unpaved street, seeing stars, trying not to pass out. Just then she felt someone lift up her skirts and rip off her knickers. One man threw his body across her face in an attempt to keep her still and quiet. She felt the rough hands of another man pull her legs apart, exposing the most private part of herself, and then cried out as a sharp stab of pain jolted her body. She was such an innocent that at first she had trouble understanding what was happening to her.

Three of them had her there in the cold of early morning and the mud of the empty street. When the first two finished, the man who had lain on her face got up.

"Don't scream," he warned, "or I'll suffocate you." To prove it, he clasped his hand over her mouth and nose and held it there, suffocating her as he took his turn at her. When he had finished, one of the others pulled out a knife. Through the haze of pain, barely holding onto consciousness, she could see the blade glinting in the moonlight and hear them discussing her fate.

"If we kill her, there'll be trouble," one of them said.

"Worse trouble if she lives," the other replied. "She might remember our faces. We'll kill her and throw her in the river."

The man with the knife nodded grimly. He walked over, put his hand on her face, tilted her head back, and lowered the knife to slice open her throat. Nelleke was too terrified to resist. She waited, paralyzed with fear, wondering what had brought this ill fortune upon her. Suddenly the man leaning over her stepped back and threw the knife he had held against her neck. She heard a noise like flint striking steel and heard the noise the knife made falling into the mud. Footsteps echoed as the three men fled.

Someone knelt and lifted her shoulders. She twisted her head to look at him. He pulled her skirts down to cover her bleeding, muddy thighs.

"Young woman, can you hear me?"

"I can hear you." When she spoke she noticed how dry her mouth was.

"I'm going to pick you up and carry you to a house where you may be cared for."

"My house," she managed to say. "Four doors down." It took all her breath to say this. She felt faint from just speaking a short sentence.

He picked her up, carried her to the door she indicated, and kicked the bottom with his foot. Her father and mother opened it.

Nelleke remembered what followed through a dim

haze of shock and disorientation. The man carried into the warmth and sanctuary of her home. Someone undressed her, washed her, and carried her to her room. She drifted into sleep and awoke to find a physician sitting beside her bed. The midwife had come with him. He examined her as the midwife and her mother stood by. When he had finished and covered her, they conferred. After what seemed like a long while, her mother returned to her bedside. She put her arms around Nelleke. Her warmth and love unleashed a flood of anguished tears from the girl. Her mother held her as she wept.

Sleep claimed her again. In the morning, her mother brought her warm bread and ale. Still in shock from last night, she stared at her food. Her mother urged her to eat. She managed to finish her breakfast and felt better, though the trauma of what had happened made her burst into hysterical tears at intervals. Her father and brothers came in to see her, and later that day the family received a visit from a magistrate and two men who looked like military officials. Nelleke described the men who had attacked her. They listened judiciously. After they left, she asked her mother about the man who had rescued her.

"His name is Izaak," she said.

"I would like to thank him. Can you call him here so I may do so?"

Her mother shook her head. "I can't. He left right after he brought you here. He didn't tell us his last name or where he lives."

"Why not?"

"He didn't say. I think he's a Jew."

Nelleke nodded. Their city tolerated Jews, but they generally kept quiet about their faith and worship. Since Protestantism had come to their land, people were more tolerant, but the war had gone well for the Spanish lately. The chance that their territory might soon be controlled by the Roman Church emboldened the partisans of that religion to rail against the Jews, saying they were behind the conflicts that had torn Europe apart that last thirty years and calling for their destruction.

Nelleke slowly recovered. The soldiers who had assaulted her were eventually identified and put on trial. Two of them were branded and imprisoned. A third, however, went free. When Nelleke's family protested, the court said he was a noble and because of his service in the forces of Utrecht had been pardoned, though he was not allowed to enter the territory formerly belonging to the City of Ijsselstein.

After the trial ended, the midwife confirmed Nelleke was pregnant.

She went into seclusion. Her family filed suit against the nobleman. The courts ruled in their favor and forced him to pay a large sum of money for the maintenance of the child and as a compensation for Nelleke.

She hated being secluded. Several of her friends called on her. Her parents turned them away.

"Mother, why do I have to live like a prisoner?" she demanded. "Why did you turn Katjie and Dorthea away? I want to see my friends."

"What happened to you was a shame and disgrace."

"You talk like it was *my* fault! *I want to see my friends!* They all know what happened. If you don't let them see me, I'll go see them myself. You can't stop me."

Her parents relented. Nelleke's friends visited. They brought her gifts, food, and assurances of their love. When Dorthea, one of her closest friends, departed after a visit one stormy morning, she left an envelope with a note in it. Nelleke locked the door and opened it. She read:

Nelleke—

My name is Izaak. I am the man who helped you.
I would like to see you again. I can help you do
justice to the man who assaulted you and went
unpunished. Leave this letter where Dorthea can
see it when she visits next week. If she returns it
to me, I'll come to see you. Also, I have your lute.
—Izaak

She contemplated. She wanted to thank him for saving her from death. Would her parents let a man in to see her? When Dorthea came to visit again, Nelleke placed the letter on her table where the two of them sat to talk and drink ale. As Dorthea left, she slipped it in into her carrying bag.

Izaak showed up two days later. Her parents showed him into the house and then retired to the kitchen so the two of them could talk in private in the main room of the house. They would be close enough to know if anything went amiss. Nelleke was six months pregnant by then. She sat in a chair by the fire, a shawl over her legs. Izaak bowed to her.

She marveled at what a magnificent man he was. He stood over six feet tall, his body slender but strong and lithe. She liked the quick, precise way moved. He had long black hair and dark eyes. Something made him look elegant even in his plain, everyday clothes.

"I thank you for saving my life," Nelleke said as the fire crackled behind her. "I heard one of the men say he meant to kill me so there would be no one to testify of their crime."

"I heard him say it as well. That was when I knew I had to intervene."

"What were you doing on our street?"

"I was returning home from an errand. Providence preserved your life. Tragedy befell you, but you are here among the living."

His words resonated with her soul. Nelleke had never been religious. She loved the stories of the Bible and liked worship, though the religious wars ravaging her country had made her dislike organized religion. Of late, her father had begun to lean toward Luther's teaching.

She invited her parents to join them. The four of them drank wine and talked. Her father asked Izaak what he did for a living. He said he inventoried warehouses and worked with the local merchants to improve their methods of counting their wares and keeping track of their holdings.

"The men who work in the warehouses steal from the owners and sell what they take on the black market," he said. "Once the warehouse owners know how to keep inventories efficiently, they're amazed at how much more money they make."

Her father commented that his line of work might make him enemies.

"Several people have lain in wait for me. I've had to fight for my life more than once."

The evening passed pleasantly. Izaak was cordial and funny. She enjoyed him being there. When he got ready to leave, he turned to her. "I have your lute. I didn't want to carry it out in the rain. I'll return it soon, I promise."

When the time came, she bore her child. A girl, strong and healthy. She named her Anita. Her beauty and the joy of a grandchild delighted her parents, but the stigma of her birth clouded their joy. Nelleke's anger rose at this. As during her pregnancy, they behaved as if she, and now the child, bore the guilt of what her assailants had done. Anita nursed well, did not sicken, grew and throve in the next few months.

When Anita turned four months old, Dorthea left her a short note. It read simply,

See me at once—Izaak

There was an address scrawled at the bottom.

Nelleke puzzled over the message. She wondered if Izaak meant to kidnap or harm her, though his behavior in rescuing her did not indicate he would do such a thing. He had risked his own life to save her. The terse, imperative style of the note expressed urgency. *If he had wanted to lure me over for evil purposes*, she thought, *he would have sent something more elaborate and flowery*. Deciding to meet him, she said she was going out for fresh air, left the baby with her mother, put on a cloak, and hurried down the streets of Ijsselstein. She came to a neat house near a wide open field.

She knocked. Izaak answered. "Nelleke. Please come in." Nelleke felt vulnerable and foolish. What had drawn her here? How could she have done such an unseemly thing? Yet the impulse that had brought her to his home remained strong. She wanted to see him. It might be sorcery and he might be the Devil, but she had to know why he had summoned her so abruptly. She had to speak with him.

The room, dimly lit, reflected marble surfaces, rich wood, and gold and silver objects. "I'll light a lamp," Izaak said. "I often forget most people don't like it as dark as I do."

He crossed the room. After some clanging and banging, he produced and lit a brass oil lamp. He turned it up so that its light illuminated the interior in which they stood.

Nelleke saw rich carpets, lovely furniture, crystal vases and silver and gold casques, candlesticks, and ornaments. A mirror hung on the wall opposite from her. She glanced for a moment at her reflection. Stairs opened at the wall opposite the mirror. *They probably lead upstairs to where he sleeps*, she thought.

"You dwell in a rich, beautiful room, sir," she

commented.

He laughed. "Please, leave off the formality. I am Izaak. And thank you."

Her eyes fell on her lute. It lay in a plush chair in one corner of the room.

"Your musical instrument," he said. "I'm sorry I didn't get it back to you sooner. Life can get complicated at times."

She picked it up. Its lacquered surface reflected lamplight. Izaak came up beside her.

"Will you play something for me?"

"I haven't played for almost a year."

"If you want to play, play. If not"—

She took up the lute, sat in the chair where it had rested, pulled the stabilizing strap under her thigh, and quickly tuned. Having not played for so long, she had lost the callous on her fingertips; still, love of the instrument took her. Her hands rested on the frets and over the sound hole. She played a folksong with a beautiful melody. The notes carried through the room, weaving their spell, wrapping her in their power. The sweetness of bringing the instrument to life charmed her. The benign sorcery she always felt when she played cast its spell on her. When she finished, she looked up at Izaak.

"Amazingly beautiful," he smiled.

"Thank you."

"How is your child?"

"She is strong and well."

"I've brought you here to talk about her. Has Sister Luke said anything to you?"

"About what?"

"About Anita."

"No." Alarm rose in her heart. "Why would she be interested in my child?"

"I have it from reliable sources that she means to take your child from you."

Nelleke stared, open-mouthed. "How? Why?"

"Sister Luke spent three years in Ireland. There, the Church takes all children born out of wedlock and puts them up for adoption."

"But I was assaulted—raped. How could they take my child—on what pretext?"

"That you are not married—for that reason alone."

Rage and fear coursed through her. "This can't be!"

"It is their policy, and they mean to enforce it."

"You had better not be making this up."

"I would not be so cruel as to make up such a thing."

Nelleke sat still, staring out and then collapsed, hiding her face in her hands. "If this is so, what can I do? How can I stand against the power of the Church?"

After a long moment of silence, Izaak said, "There is a way."

She looked up. "Why are you doing this? Are you trying to manipulate me?"

"Perhaps I am."

"I've been abused enough as it is."

"True. We'll take up the subject at a later date. Now you need to return home."

He escorted her back. When she arrived, she found her daughter safely asleep in her crib. Her parents wanted to know where she had been. Understandably, they were anxious to about her going out alone. And they noticed she had her missing lute.

"I visited Izaak, the young man who rescue me. He told me he had my lute when he visited the other day. I decided to get it from him. I suppose I should have told you, but I wanted to go for a walk and get some fresh air. He lives in a busy neighborhood. I was not in any danger."

They told her she needed to be careful.

III

No one attempted to take Anita from her. She grew angry at Izaak. How dare he make up such a tale? How dare he frighten her? She wondered at his motive and at what he had meant when he said he might perhaps be trying to manipulate her.

A month after they had spoken, she came down from nursing her child who, after two quiet lullabies, had gone to sleep. Fear filled her when she saw Sister Luke and a younger nun, the Magistrate, and her parents all seated in the front room of their house. Her mouth went dry. The Magistrate opened his mouth to speak, but Nelleke interdicted whatever he had meant to say by declaring, "You're here to take my child."

"Nelleke," her father said.

She turned to rush up the stairs. Her father caught her arm and restrained her. "I'll kill you," Nelleke screamed, wheeling about and pointing at Sister Luke. "I'll cut your heart out and piss on your grave after they bury you!"

Her insult to Sister Luke frightened everyone else in the room, but the nun spoke up, her voice even, her expression beatific.

"Child, we knew you would be upset"—

"You haven't seen me upset!"

Nelleke almost mentioned Izaak—his kindness and courage—but refrained.

"The child," the Magistrate intoned judiciously, "will be placed in a good home where she can have a father and a mother."

"I won't let you take her," Nelleke screamed. She began to struggle. The Magistrate called in two men who had apparently been waiting outside. They and Nelleke's father carried her into the kitchen and held her there. She screamed and raged. When she heard Anita crying as they carried her out, she went into a paroxysm, stiffening and foaming at the mouth. She woke up in bed. Her mother told her it was two days since Anita was taken away.

All day she lay in bed and stared at the wall. She would not eat. She contemplated withdrawing into herself so she would not have to face the impossible world without the child of her womb. She might have done so, but then she remembered what Izaak had said. That evening she told her mother she wanted something to eat.

As she ate, she contemplated. He had admitted he was manipulating her, though the tone of his voice and the way he phrased his answer had puzzled her. But whatever Izaak wanted from her, she would give it to him. She would do anything to get her child.

When her mother was busy cooking, Nelleke threw on a cloak, silently left the house, made her way through rain mixed with snow to Izaak's house, and knocked. He opened the door and received her. His smile was sad. He knew. After hanging up her coat on a peg and helped her take off her boots, he gave her cider to drink. They sat in silence for a time. Nelleke listened to the crackling of the fire. Finally, she spoke.

"I'll do anything to get Anita back. If you want me to yield my body to you, I will—as often as you want and with no blame or reproach on you. I have money from the settlement with the Marquis. I'll give you that or anything else I have. I just want my child."

"I will get your child back for you."

"How will you do that?"

"Let's say I have my ways. I will get the child and hide her until I can arrange to get you to a place where you can raise her. After that, the only promise I ask is that you will hear what I have to say. But not before your child is freed."

She nodded, unable to speak. "Could I have more cider?" she asked after a long silence.

He refilled her cup. She felt safe in his house. The cider, good and strong, relaxed her. The warm house where he lived radiated charm. Dark wood, red fabric, gold and silver and crystal suggested safety and refuge. He sat near her and sipped his drink. After a while, she said something she would have not thought herself capable of uttering.

"I want to stay with you tonight."

His eyes meet hers. She read surprise in them.

"Well, of course. I can fix a bed for you down here, but won't your parents wonder where you are?"

"They will. As soon as I go home, I'll tell them I was with a friend."

"That might not be wise."

"I'm tired of being wise. I tried to live a life of wisdom and look what it got me. I can't face my parents tonight."

He nodded slowly. As Nelleke waited, he went upstairs and returned with blankets and a pad. He made her a bed by the fireplace, smiled, nodded, and went upstairs. Exhausted, Nelleke undressed and climbed under the quilts.

He roused her before the sun was up and said they needed to get her home.

"I can't go home yet. Anyway, I won't able to get in."

"I'll get you in."

They came to Nelleke's house in the dark before sunrise. Nelleke's parents' bedroom lay on the side of the house away from the street. They would not hear her knock. Izaak told her to wait by the door and hurried away.

Snow fell in large flakes. It lay deep in the streets. Jitze, their serving man, would be busy shoveling in a few hours. After only moments, the door opened. Izaak beckoned her to enter.

"How did you get inside?"

"I'll explain that and much more soon."

She went to her bedroom and fell asleep immediately.

IV

The next day, Dorthea came and gave Nelleke an address. The two of them rendezvoused by Saint Simon's Church. Dorthea emerged from the church with a book in her hands. Nelleke wanted to know why Dorthea had summoned her and if she had heard anything about Anita, but she held back the anxiety in her heart. She noticed the titles printed on the outside of the books.

"Latin?" she asked.

"Yes. I'm learning to read Latin and to speak French and English," she said. "The nuns are teaching me."

"Do you have a vocation toward religion?" Nelleke knew the nuns who favored that church taught languages, but only to girls who planned to enter the convent.

She smiled, looked about her, and lowered her voice. "Nelleke, are you that much of a goose? I'm a Jew. My family pretends to be Christian so we won't be mistreated."

This astonished Nelleke—but then, she thought, it explained her connection with Izaak. They walked along in silence, making their way through the city, coming at last to the ghetto. They passed the pillars that had held the gates in the days when the city officials closed the place up every night and kept the Jews confined because people thought they came out during the darkness hours to do evil. No one believed that anymore. City officials had taken down the gates. Restrictions on the Jews had relaxed over the years, though from time to time friars or nuns would try to whip up hostility against them. That kind of fanaticism did not win much sympathy with the people of Ijsselstein, who did business with the Jews and considered them worthy citizens.

The two young women came to a house. Dorthea knocked in a certain pattern. The door opened. The woman who opened it let them in without a greeting. Once inside, they walked up a flight of stairs to a bedroom. Izaak stood there, a quiet smile on his face. On the bed, bare expect for a diaper, lay Anita.

Nelleke gasped, squealed, and took her child in her arms. Anita wept at first but then began to coo and laugh. She knew her mother. Nelleke rocked her and gave her her breast, thankful her milk had not stopped. As Anita sucked hungrily, Nelleke softly cried. No one, she resolved, would ever take her child from her again.

Anita eventually dozed off. Nelleke held her, rocking the child, not wanting to let go of her. The room, she noticed, was dark. A thick black curtain covered the window. Lamps burned in the hallway. She remembered how bright it was outside.

"Thank you," she said, her voice flat because she wanted to keep emotion back. "Thank you, Izaak. What can I do now?"

"I'll tell you in two weeks."

"Tell me now. I don't want to wonder what your plan is. I'm tired of waiting to know. Tell me now."

He met her eyes. She could tell from his gaze he did not want to talk but knew he had to. Anita stirred.

"Sit down. I'll tell you everything."

He explained. When he finished, she stared at him. Words would not form. He smiled.

"You think I'm mad?"

She managed to say, "You must be." Immediately, however, her mind went to Anita. He seemed to read her thoughts.

"No harm will come to your child or to you."

"How can I believe you?"

"What I've done for you so far so should show that you are not in any danger. I am obligated to you because I saved your life. I am under oath now to protect you."

"For the evil purpose that drives you?" she asked, thinking of how much vampire stories had horrified and frightened her as a child.

"No."

"Is Dorthea one of your kind?"

"If she were, she could not go out in the light. She is one of many who know of us. We protect her."

"From what?"

"From evil. From oppression and injustice."

"How did you free Anita?"

"Vampires are very good at getting in places—especially at night. You saw how I got inside your house to open the door for you."

"How can you slay innocent people? Don't you feel remorse for that?"

"I don't kill innocent people. My family strikes only the guilty."

"Family?"

"There are clans of vampires. We have laws and traditions. My family only strikes at those who are evil, who cause death and misery and oppress the innocent. There are those who prey on the innocent, it's true. Our clan does not do so."

Nelleke did not know what to say. She still through Izaak might be deranged. He looked glum.

"I'll hate to see you go," he said.

"Who said I want to go?"

"There is no way you can be safe here. To raise your child, you'll have to leave the country. England might be the best place. We can arrange for you to go there and give you a place to stay. You'll be too far from the authorities for them to discover you—and if you stay anywhere in Holland, they will eventually find you. Also, you speak the language. That will be to your advantage. You can help Dorthea."

When Nelleke's family had lived in Rotterdam, her father sold merchandise to the English. He had taught her the language and, with a child's alacrity, she picked it up and still spoke it well even though they had moved inland three years ago. The local merchants in Ijsselstein relied on her as a translator when they did business transactions with the English.

"I thought Dorthea was learning English."

"She is, but she doesn't speak it well."

"What will she do to support herself?"

"She's marrying one of our clan."

"She is? How can that be?"

"She'll become one of us."

Horror struck her. Her mouth fell open. "Become a vampire?" she echoed, eyes round with astonishment and fear. "How could this be? Why would anyone want to become one of the undead—become a creature that preys on other and repasts on their blood?"

He answered with an even voice. Nelleke could see in his eyes that what she had said offended him.

"No one is born this way. There are two ways to become one of the undying. You can be bitten by a vampire. Most who are bitten die. Some become vampires—very few, only one out of ten thousand. Our folk immediately know when this happens and assist those who cross over—that's what we call it—in their new life."

He stopped. Nelleke's throat felt dry. "What is the other way? What's going to happen to Dorthea?"

"I'm not allowed to tell you."

"Dorthea is the most gentle, kind woman in the world.

How could you do this to her? How could you make her into a monster?"

Izaak winced at the word she used. Still, he did not let his anger at what she said color his response.

"She requested it," he answered. "Personally, I don't think it's a good idea. I would not curse anyone—even my worst enemy—with the life we are forced to live. But she desires it and her request has been approved by our leaders. You need to ask her about it."

Disoriented by the unreal, insane talk she had heard, Nelleke, could only nod. She and Izaak sat in silence for a long time. Finally, when her thought began to stir again, she thought of Anita sleeping upstairs and asked, "When will I leave for England?"

"A ship is departing in three days. You don't need to take anything. You'll have a place to stay—you and little Anita and can begin life over there."

A distressing silence came.

"Will I ever see you again?"

He opened his mouth—to lie, she saw—but then he thought better of it.

"I suppose I could see you after all my obligations here are fulfilled. That would be in a few months."

"I hope we'll see each other again. I owe so much to you."

After another half hour spent in silence, trying to sort out the unbelievable things she had encountered but knew must be true, Nelleke allowed Izaak to walk her home. Her mother chided her for being gone. She only said it helped her to take the fresh air.

Over the next two weeks, Nelleke selected the items she would take with her to England and hid them in a bag under her bed. No one came to her home to question her about Anita's absence. She supposed no one noticed the child was gone. Every woman at the orphanage where they had taken her probably thought someone else was caring for her, Nelleke surmised. At dusk on the appointed day she sneaked off and hid in Izaak's apartment. She gave a local boy two silver pieces to deliver a letter to the parents the day after she was gone. On the day of departure, she met up with Dorthea. The two of them made their way to the edge of town and climbed into the back of a wagon. A woman in the back had brought Anita. As Nelleke nursed her child, the wagon rumbled forward and she asked Dorthea how she could ever desire to become a ghoul who lived by drinking the blood of other people.

"I'm in love," she said simply.

"With whom?"

'His name is Bernard. I met him when I visited London once." Dorthea's father was also a merchant. "We fell in love. When he told me we could never be lovers, I demanded to know why. He wouldn't tell me, but I kept after him. He couldn't run from me because he did business with my father and had to be present for the various deals they were making. Then I noticed he never came out in the sun and transacted business deals in a darkened room. I already knew about Izaak. I asked if he were a vampire. He said he was. I told him I didn't care."

"But vampires are... well, I don't want to say, but what they must do to stay alive is horrible and destructive."

"'What they must do' explains it all. They didn't ask to be vampires, Nelleke."

"But *you're* asking to be one!"

"I suppose I am. I'm willing to do that for the sake of love. Bernard belongs to Izaak's clan. He only preys on people who are evil."

Nelleke remembered what Izaak had told her and

reflected on how he had helped her. Vampires were capable of good. The paradoxes confused her. Yet she knew she was alive and had her kidnapped child back because of him.

"Dorthea, please don't. For the love of all that is good and true, don't do this."

"I'm doing it for love," Dorthea answered, her voice full of emotion, "and if love isn't good and true, I don't know what is. Izaak saved your life and gave you back your child. He's a vampire. Is he evil? The Bible says you can know an evil person by their fruit—by what they do and what they produce in their life. Izaak has done so much good for you. The question isn't as simple as you're making it, Nelleke."

Nelleke quieted down. Dorthea sat there trying not to cry. Nelleke took her hand. She didn't want to offend her best friend from childhood. And what Dorthea had said—Nelleke would have to ponder it. They sat in silence and held hands all the way to the coast.

Other than this discussion, the trip from Ijsselstein to Rotterdam was without drama. They hid out when they arrived there. Word came that the nobleman who raped her had been killed and that the baby born out of the incident had disappeared. Nelleke and Dorthea hid in fear and did not relax until the British ship they boarded pulled away from the Dutch shore and made its way toward England, putting miles of water between them and what had been their native country.

They arrived at Weymouth after a calm voyage with good winds and checked through customs. Their permissions to enter England had already been secured; Nelleke, Anita, and Dorthea boarded a wagon and started north and west for Devonshire.

When night drew on, they stayed at an inn, where they shared a room and a bed and paid for a crib for Anita. In the morning they renewed their journey. At the end of four days, they stopped near dusk at a farmhouse set in a rocky, thickly wooded corner of the shire.

Nelleke and Dorthea were dusty, tired, and sore. Anita cried. A servant girl helped them inside. They washed and changed into clean clothes. After Anita was bathed and nursed, she fell asleep. The two women sat before the hearth and sipped wine. The serving woman prepared a meal. They had rested perhaps fifteen minutes when the door opened and a figure came through the door. Dorthea put down her goblet, rushed to him, and threw her arms around him. Nelleke smiled. Her smile turned to a gasp of disbelief when she saw Izaak enter just after him.

She rushed over, embraced him, and asked him what he was doing here.

"Something changed," he said. "Dorthea will be brought into the community tonight. We were going to wait a few months, but the head of the Council plans to do it right away."

"How is this done?"

"I can't tell you. We can't tell anyone, even people we trust."

"Is it... I mean, is it... terrible?"

He smiled. "It most certainly is, but what it entails is even more terrible."

"How could that be? You're bringing her into your community and she wants to be a part of it."

"I tried to talk her out of it many times. It's not as wonderful as she assumes it will be. You never die. Most people dream of such a life, but I often think death would be preferable to endless existence."

"How could that be? You live forever."

"It's not as wonderful as it sounds."

"No one wants to die. I don't." She hesitated, and then asked, "How many years have you lived, Izaak? Will you tell me?"

"I've lived two hundred years. I'm 'young' for a vampire.

I was bitten one night and entered the coven. At first, I thought living forever would be a dream come true. But I saw my family and my friends all die while I lived on."

"That would be sad, but you're still alive," she said, seeing the look of sadness in his eyes.

"Maybe we're meant to die. Maybe it's the right thing to do."

They stood in awkward silence. Wanting to move from such a morbid subject, Izaak said, "Anita is such a beautiful child."

Nelleke nodded. She was growing too sleepy to talk.

She shared a bed with Dorthea again that night. When day broke, Nelleke took Anita out for a walk in the morning sun. When she came back, Dorthea was making breakfast.

"I want you to come to my initiation into the community, Nelleke."

"Izaak said I couldn't—that outsiders were not allowed to attend."

"Normally, the living are not allowed. But there have been exceptions. I want you to be there."

"Why?"

"Because I love you. Because you're my best friend. And I want you to see the ceremony."

"Izaak said it was"—

"It will be a little bit gruesome, yes. But I want you to be there because I love you. I want us to be friends even if we belong to different worlds. I've asked the leader of our coven and he gave me permission. Please, Nelleke."

She breathed in to steady herself and then nodded.

The house where the ceremony would be held looked like any other one might find in the woodland rides of the province. Built of heavy squared-off logs with a thatched room and a stone chimney, it sat in a clearing surrounded on all sides by tall trees. Two or three smaller structures stood around it. Dim light showed through the windows, which were not glass but covered with what looked like very thin animal skins. Nelleke and Izaak reined in the horses they were riding, dismounted, took the saddles and bridles from their mounts, set them to graze in a fenced-off pasture, and went inside. A guard at the door stopped them. He cast a stern look at Nelleke.

"We have permission," Izaak told him.

The guard eyed Nelleke. He was an older man with long grey hair and piercing black eyes. "You'd better stay close to her," he advised in a gravelly voice. "This is a big group, and we have a lot of wodies. She needs to be careful."

They made their way inside.

"What's a 'wodie'?" she whispered.

"I'll tell you later. And don't pay any attention to what he said about their being rough. Actually, they're kind and benevolent. He's a city-dweller and is a little bit bigoted about the wodies."

The interior of the house formed one large room, like a meeting hall. A raised podium stood in the front. Torches blazed. A central fire burned. Its flames shone silver, not yellow and orange. Wooden benches filled the front. Izaak directed her to sit.

Once seated, she looked about her. She counted twenty others in the room. She was surprised to see more women than men (twelve women, eight men) and also that some of the figures around the fire were so young. Two of the men and two of the women looked not much older than fifteen. If vampires lived forever and did not age, she reasoned, they must remain fixed at the age they changed from humans. Did they attack children? She shuddered to think of it. Some of the vampires dressed normally, but some wore garments

26

made of animal skins and looked rough and wild. Were these the "wodies" Izaak had mentioned? She snuggled closer to him and took his hand.

Dorthea and her fiancé walked up to the podium. She wore a simple blue smock, had untied her hair, and was barefoot. A tall, pale man with long blond hair stepped on to the podium and stood near the front. He wore expensive clothes and a long cape. Something about him made Nelleke uneasy. He turned and nodded to Dorthea and her fiancé Bernard (his real name was Barak).

"We have gathered to receive a soul," the blond man said.

The group of vampires responded, "We have gathered to receive a soul." They spoke in unison, almost in a chant. Nelleke perceived this was a litany for the ceremony.

At a signal from the man conducting the ceremony. Bernard reached over and removed Dorthea's garment.

Nelleke winced with shock to see her best friend stripped naked in front of so many watching eyes. She had slept and bathed with Nelleke many times, and knew her nakedness. She felt embarrassed to see her stripped like this and see what was most sacred and designed to be hidden exposed for everyone to see. Yet Nelleke thought her friend looked beautiful and exquisite in the dimness of the room. Her light skin, long golden hair, slender and beautiful body seemed lonely and vulnerable. Her small, lovely breasts, long legs and arms, the wisp of light brown hair between her legs made her look innocent. Her eyes showed fear but also love for Bernard.

"Dorthea, do you consent to this?" the man in the cape asked. Izaak managed to whisper to Nelleke that his name was Anmur, he had lived a thousand years, and was the leader of the vampire coven in south England.

"I do."

"Willingly?"

"Willingly, my Lord."

The man nodded. Bernard took a dagger from his pocket. It reflected the silver firelight.

Nelleke had imagined there might be an exchange of blood. He would cut her, she would cut him, and they would mingle their blood like she had read the natives of the Americas sometimes did. Bernard stood a moment, looking into Dorthea's eyes. She nodded. The knife flashed as he drew it across her throat.

Nelleke gasped, trying to keep from screaming. Izaak took her hand and squeezed it to assure her. A dark stream of blood ran down from Dorthea's neck to her breasts. Nelleke wanted to look away or close her eyes but could not. She stared with horror as the red cascade ran over her body. She swayed, her legs unsteady. The wave of blood spread downward toward her stomach and thighs. Nelleke suppressed the impulse to go to her. Would no one intervene? Did they simply mean to let her die? Anmur caught Dorthea's limp body and held her up. Bernard slashed his hand. He touched his bleeding palm to her throat.

To Nelleke's amazement, the cloak of blood around Dorthea's body began to disappear, as if her flesh had absorbed it. She stared in amazement as the red faded and then disappeared. Dorthea became steadier on her feet. Anmur let go of her. Her eyes opened and cleared. The expression of pain on her face faded. She stood there, naked, no trace of blood on her body. Nelleke noticed the blood on Bernard's hand and wrist had also vanished. Bernard reached back, picked up the smock, and helped her on with it. All the vampires stood and recited something in a language Nelleke did not understand. After the liturgy ended, the mood lightened and then turned festive. The creatures applauded, shouted out good wishes, smiled and rejoiced. Dorthea looked exhausted and sat down in a chair someone brought to the podium, and as Nelleke observed her she thought she saw something different in her eyes—a glint not exactly evil but suggesting she saw a new vision. She knew what the other vampires knew. She understood. She was one of their fellowship.

Nelleke felt her status as an outsider even more acutely. She moved closed to Izaak.

The vampires continued to applaud and shout in triumph at receiving Dorthea into their company, though the celebration seemed subdued to Nelleke. The male and female vampires went up to embrace Anne and Bernard and speak with them. She wondered if she should go. Izaak leaned down and whispered that by their laws, she could go up and touch Dorthea but must not speak to her.

"A silly rule and no one knows why we have it," he said, "but it is enforced."

Nelleke shuddered to think what *enforced* might mean. She and Izaak found their way into the line of well-wishers. Izaak approached Dorthea and kissed, saying, "Welcome." She smiled. Nelleke touched her face and, after a moment of hesitation, kissed her. No scar lay where Bernard had cut her; the flesh of her neck showed smooth and fair as before. Nelleke did not speak. She and her friend shared a smile. Dorthea squeezed Nelleke's hand and they parted.

Izaak told her there would be a celebration. They walked to one of the smaller houses nearby. Unlike the dwelling they had left, it was lit dimly with candles. This house, however, contained furniture: a table and chairs. Inside, a banquet had been set out. Nelleke gathered food, wondering why vampires needed food if they drank blood. She sat down at the table, looking for Izaak. One of the rough-looking vampire women settled beside her. Nelleke glanced at her, noting her strong arms, long, wild locks, calloused hands, legs covered with curly black hair, and bare feet. The woman smiled.

"Greetings," she said. "I am Arabella."

"Nelleke," she replied, a little afraid.

The woman laughed. "You're Izaak's love."

Nelleke looked at her. "Love?"

The woman laughed. "Well, it's rumored you love him, whether you do or not. We all think a great deal of Izaak, and whether you love him are not, you are a fortunate young woman to be in his company. Be careful, though. A lot of the women here are jealous you became the one for him."

Nelleke could not tell if the woman was teasing her or spoke seriously. She hardly qualified as his love. But at that moment, she felt a pang in her heart. Could others see what she had not allowed herself to admit? Not wanting to think of this, she thanked Arabella and said she was happy to meet her.

They fell to the feast before them. Arabella ate with gusto, but her manners were not gross or unseemly. Her eating suggested vigor, strength, and energy. After a time, Nelleke decided to ask her a question that had played on her mind since Izaak mentioned it.

"Are you a 'wodie?'" she asked.

Arabella looked over at her. "I am, child."

"What does it mean to be that?"

She laughed. "We live in the woodlands and drink the blood of animals. We don't kill humans for food. The others consider us savages and dolts, but we have our lives and are content with them. I can't imagine living in the filth and squalor of a city." Arabella studied Nelleke a moment. "You are a most comely human," she observed, "and you have the love of our Izaak. Whether he says so or not, he loves you. I've known him for a hundred years and can tell when he is smitten by a lovely woman—and, believe me, he is in love with you. Have you thought of doing what Dorthea did?"

Nelleke blushed. In the flash of a moment, she realized she had, in unguarded moments, considered the possibility—which told her Arabella was right about Izaak loving her and that she herself had seen the same thing and, in her heart, begun to respond. Though she had not allowed the notion to enter her head as an articulate though, in the recesses of her heart, in the secret place of her spirit, she was in love with Izaak.

"I have a child. I want to raise her without the... *complications* Izaak and the rest of you face."

"Who is the father of your child?"

"I don't know," Nelleke said, and then for the first time ever, she told her story. Arabella listened, taking her hand when emotion overcame Nelleke. She managed to tell her story to the end and saw tears in Arabella's eyes. Her weather-beaten but beautiful face radiated sympathy.

"I'm so sorry for what befell you," she said, giving Nelleke a small hug. She smelled of pine trees and the open air. "When I entered the world of the undead, I had two children. I knew I could not properly raise them if I could not live in daylight."

"What did you do?"

"I gave them to some of the folk who live in the woods and they raised them. I was able to see my son and daughter as often as I wanted—at night, of course—or on stormy days when the sun did not shine."

"That sounds terrible. Was there no way you could have kept them yourself?"

"Remember that I lived in the country. In the city, our people have found ways to raise children safely. If had stayed in London or Exeter or Oxford, I could have had my children in my own care, but I was a fugitive from justice. King Henry's agents were everywhere watching for me, so I had to hide in the woods, where our people were not able to help me very much with the care of my son and daughter. If I had not been pursued, things might have been different— easier. But I did what I had to do, painful though it was."

"I'm sorry, Arabella. Do the wood dwellers know..."

"They do, but they also know we don't feed on humans. We protect them and they provide us with things we can't find in the forest—tools, utensils, cloth."

"What do you protect them from?"

"Wild animals—wolves mostly. But we also protect them from rapacious landowners who would tax and exploit them. The landowners have been told savage eaters of human flesh live in the area—vampires who would repast on their blood—not entirely true, but what they don't know won't hurt them. And when they do venture the woodlands, we manage to frighten them so they stay away."

"You speak well," Nelleke said. She stopped, wondering if she had made a blunder. Arabella only smiled.

"I am not a country woman. I lived at the court of Henry VIII. I was a lady-in-waiting for Anne Boleyn. When she fell out of favor and was sentenced to die, custom dictated that one of her serving women die with her. The lot fell to me. I fled here. I was bitten and joined the ranks of the undying."

Nelleke drank wine with Arabella until Izaak joined them. A fiddler and cittern player struck up a melody. She and Izaak danced. It seemed odd to see vampires dance— and there was something somber about their merriment. She supposed it would have to be that way if you were dead. The love that had grown in her heart, the budding affection she had denied, began to quietly blaze. She could not deny it now—love and the obligation she felt to him for saving her life and rescuing her child. She danced close to him and, despite her knowledge of how he killed to keep himself alive, felt safe with him.

The party grew livelier. The several cups of wine she had shared with Arabella had their effect and Nelleke danced, laughed, and accepted a mug of ale and two small cups of whisky. A little drunk, she went outside to use the privy.

When she neared the outdoor toilet, something struck her on the back. The blow knocked the breath from her. She fell and immediately felt something clawing at her. She screamed and then felt a sharp pain on the side of the neck.

The pain coursed through her but abruptly stopped. A dizzy, unequal sensation gripped her, as if she were spiraling downward, falling from a great height; as if she were drowning and sinking; as if a gentle fire had burned her insides away and filled her with bliss and with the desire to run, to leap, to hunt. She opened her eyes to see a disheveled woman kneeling over her, a horrified look on her face. She heard noises and shouting. The woman sprang up.

Nelleke rolled to one side. Her neck hurt, but the sensation coursing through her body took her attention from the pain. A fire coursed through her veins and an indescribable music rang in her mind. *I must be going mad,* she thought.

She saw the woman who had been standing over her run toward the privy. A second later, Arabella leaped over her. Running as fast as a deer, she closed in on the fleeing woman. As Nelleke watched, the woman who had knocked her down and bit her held up her arms and—she gasped even in her pain and confusion—turned into a black shape with wings—a crow or bat—and flapped twice, rising into the air. Arabella rushed up, leaping, caught her by the wings, and pulled her down.

"Bitch!" Arabella shouted. "Change back or I'll tear you in two!"

By now the other vampires were running and shouting all around Nelleke. Izaak knelt by her side.

"Nelleke!"

She managed to lift her arm and rub the wound on her neck.

"What happened?"

He put his arms around her and lifted her. She cried out

in pain. As she did she heard pleading and cursing. In spite of a sharp smarting in her neck and shoulder, she twisted her head and could see Arabella holding the woman's arm in a strong grip. Several other vampires had laid hands on her. They were cursing her and calling her vile names.

After a moment, Anmur, the man who had officiated at Anne's induction into the vampire world, appeared. Dorthea walked a little ways behind him.

By now things had quieted down. Anmur strode up to where Arabella and the others had secured the woman. After a moment, Anmur spoke.

"Eseld," he said. "I didn't think you would be stupid enough to come stalking around here." He glanced back at Nelleke and Izaak. "You must have been hungry. Looks like your plans backfired."

The pain in Nelleke's neck and shoulder seemed to be fading.

"Take her inside, Izaak," Anmur ordered. He turned back to the woman. "Get her in, too. Be sure she doesn't get away. Hurt her. She might try to mist." (Nelleke would later find out vampires could not only turn into bats but transform to mist, and if a vampire was hurt by another vampire, they could not transform until they healed, which usually took several hours).

As Nelleke watched, Arabella seized the woman— Eseld's—arm and with one violent motion, broke it. Nelleke heard it snap. Eseld screamed and crumpled to her knees. Her captors pulled her up and dragged her toward the house. Izaak held Nelleke gently. "Come on," he said.

He helped her back to the house, though now she felt strong again. Her wound, which had caused her so much pain only minutes ago, seemed to have completely healed. The strange sensations she felt frightened and exhilarated her.

Izaak led her to a chair. Anmur walked over and

examined the wound.

"We weren't expecting this," he told Izaak. Izaak shook his head. Anmur turned to the captive Eseld.

"I don't see any reason to delay," he said, his voice flat, his eyes cold. "Get her ready."

Arabella and another vampire pulled off Eseld's garment. Three of the men and Arabella held her fast. Anmur went to a box toward the rear of the podium and took out a long wooden stake. Eseld began to scream and plead as he approached her. In response to her frantic cries for mercy, the vampires – especially Arabella the wodie – looked at her with contempt and smiles of cruelty. Anmur stood before Eseld a moment and then drove the wooden stake deep into her body where her heart beat.

She screamed in a loud, unearthly voice. The howl diminished into nothing and, as Nelleke gaped, Eseld's body began to change. Her flesh suddenly desiccated, its tone changing to a dull, dingy brown that radiated out from where the stake had entered her body. The dull color spread and parts of her body seemed to fall away. Nelleke suddenly realized the woman was turning to dust—to dry, brown dirt. The transformation coursed over her body. Her limbs disintegrated and what had been her form fell to pieces, a small cloud rising as she came apart, the shape of her torso collapsing in chunks. In a moment, a heap of dust lay where the woman had stood.

Nelleke turned her bewildered eyes on Izaak. At that moment Anmur walked over to them.

"At least this part of the affair had a happy ending—or I assume it's happy," he said, his voice gruff even in talk about a happy ending. "What now, Izaak?"

"I'll be her angel," he said. Anmur nodded and walked away.

"What happened?" Nelleke whispered. Izaak picked her up, sat in the chair, and lowered Nelleke onto his lap.

"Several things. Eseld was a criminal. Anmur—all of us, really—had been pursuing her for years."

"What did she do?"

"I'll tell you later. For the present"—he stopped. She looked up at him with big eyes. He sighed. "Nelleke, you're one of us now," he said. "You've become a vampire."

V

The house had been carefully shuttered to block the daylight the day before in anticipation of Dorthea becoming a vampire. Now Nelleke found shelter there as well. She and Dorthea were mostly quiet about the transformation the two of them had undergone. At dusk, a knock came at the door and Dorthea let Izaak inside. He took Nelleke aside and expressed his sorrow at her unplanned turning. "But now," he added, "there is no way to reverse it."

"Exactly how did it happen? Last night is a bit of a blur; everything went by so quickly and unexpectedly."

"When a vampire bites a person, normally the person dies," Izaak told her. "But not everyone. One person out of thousands becomes one of us. We don't know how, but it happens. I came into the world of the undying this way. Most of us do. Very few people choose to join our numbers. Now you're among us."

"It fits," she said, her voice bitter. "I'm raped. I get pregnant. People try to take my child and I have to flee my homeland and my family. Now this. Will I have to kill people and drink their blood?" She shuddered at the very thought of it.

"Yes. And soon."

She wanted to say she would rather die but remembered Anita.

"How can I raise my child?" she lamented.

"It might be done. Arabella raised her children."

"She gave her children to other people and let those people raise them. She could only see them at night. I could never do so with Anita."

"Vampires have found ways to raise children since then. Now that you're a member of the community you can ask some of our numbers who have done that."

"How can I raise a child if I only can go out at night? What happens if I go out in the sun?"

"You'll die—in great agony. You are among us now and we'll teach you how to live."

She felt as wretched as when she had been raped. Despair rolled over her. Izaak clasped her hand.

"You have a community of people who care about you—people who love you. We didn't mean this to happen. I didn't want it to happen."

"I don't want to be a vampire," she wept. "I don't. God help me!"

"You have no choice now. The transformation has already taken place and there is nothing you can do to change that."

Nelleke wept. But despite her panic and despair, she sensed a terrible bonding to Izaak—not from the love she had begun to feel for him; it came from something else—something growing in her soul, assuaging her pain and, as she felt it more strongly, turning her away from hopelessness. She wondered at it.

He leaned closer to her. "You feel the way you feel," he said, "because you are accepting your new identity. And also because you need blood. Your body is crying for it."

All day long Nelleke had felt a vague uneasy energy coursing through her, preventing her from resting, making her tense and uneasy. As she realized it was the thirst for blood, she burst into a new round of despairing wails. Even in her anguish, though, she knew she had to satisfy the dull, gnawing impulses surging inside her.

"I'll take you hunting," Izaak said. "Let me go get Arabella and she can talk to you while I do some scouting."

She nodded. She wanted to know what Arabella had meant about how vampires had found ways to raise children. Izaak left the room. After a few moments, Arabella came in, sat down by the bed, took Nelleke's fingers, and kissed them.

"Child, I am so sorry."

Nelleke looked at her. Something about her strength and her wildness seemed reassuring. Her long auburn hair flowed in profusion over her shoulders and over the dark brown of the buckskin garment she wore. Her face, her strong arms and hands were weather-beaten. The dress she wore, short, came above her well-shaped knees; hair covered her powerful legs (Nelleke had begun to shave her legs as fashion dictated now). Arabella's bare feet, with splayed toes, dark from treading the forest, made her look solid and firmly placed.

"How were you able to raise your child?" Nelleke asked. "How? How can I?"

"Remember, the night belongs to you. During the day you must stay inside. You'll learn to accommodate the currents of light and dark. And you have Izaak to be your teacher. You can see your child during the dark hours. But if you return to London—are you planning to do this?—"

"I imagine I will."

"—If you return to London, there are women who know of us and who can be trusted to care for your child doing the day. Clarice and Tristana will help you. You will not need to abandon Anita."

She muttered "Thank God," but felt what she had uttered odd and inappropriate. Increasingly, God seemed to have less and less to do with things. Then she felt suddenly curious. "What happened to you husband?" she asked.

"I was a widow. My husband died in the wars against

France."

"Can I drink the blood of animals as you do?"

"You can—but it will not work for you unless you choose to live in the woods where you can easily find animals as Roger and I do. This is because the blood of animals will not sustain you as long as the blood of a human being will and you must hunt more often. If you try to live in the city, hunting animals as often as you will need to will be impractical—impossible, I would say."

"How long will human blood sustain me?"

"A month—sometimes two. You'll only need to hunt and eat once a month or every other month if you choose human victims. The blood of an animal will sustain you only a week. I live where deer and other beasts abound. If you wish to live from the creatures of the wild, it is necessary to live where they can easily be found."

Nelleke pondered this. Arabella waited patiently through her long silence.

"Who was Eseld?"

"Eseld was a criminal. She lured one of my children by saying she had a message from me. My children had seen us together and trusted her. Eseld killed my daughter to satisfy her hunger. And she violated the covenant our community maintains in many other ways."

"That's horrible. I'm so sorry, Arabella."

"The loss of my child is a pain that will never leave my heart. Now that Eseld is dead, I feel some satisfaction, but the pain is there and will be for all time."

Nelleke said nothing. "I must go," Arabella said. "I must return to my cottage before the sun rises. Rest assured that you will be able to raise your child and not have to give her to others to raise, as I did with my son and daughter. And I think Izaak needs to take you hunting soon."

She nodded. Arabella squeezed her hand and left.

Nelleke nursed Anita and put her to bed. She still had

milk, which amazed her. And her body still functioned. She breathed, felt her heart beat, had to relieve herself in the privy, and wanted food as well—though eating some flesh and drinking wine did not erase the gnawing feeling in her heart that Izaak had identified as thirst for blood.

One of the women who had been at Dorthea's initiation promised to watch Anita. Izaak returned from "scouting." He and Nelleke went into the night to hunt.

Nelleke wondered how they could find someone "bad." Did Izaak plan his forays into the night with certain people in mind? If he only killed harmful, evil men and women, did he select his victims based on reports of their actions? These things ran through her mind, but the hunger she felt displaced them. She found herself thinking of nothing else but the satisfaction her body sought. Izaak glanced at her as the two of them walked along the forest road.

"I also need to eat," he said. "I have some people in mind."

She could not reply. The hunger she felt had by now pushed her to the point of near madness.

Nelleke and Izaak went deeper into the dark of the woods. Surprise filled Nelleke that she could see. Then she remembered Izaak saying something about vampires being able to see in the dark.

Scuffling, swishing noises came to her ears. In a moment they were surrounded by four rough-looking men. They held torches and carried knives; one had a pistol. A man holding a torch approached them. His leering smile revealed a set of rotten teeth.

"Well now," he said. Nelleke had trouble understanding his accent. "This is luck to come across some wealthy travelers we can rob. They wear fine clothes and no doubt have gold in their purses. Nice boots the lady is wearing." As he looked at Nelleke, his smile turned to an evil leer. "And we'll all have a nice piece of pussy to round things out! This is going to be a good night."

After a moment of silence, Izaak swiped at the man who had spoken, hitting him with such force he flew through the air, his torch careening into the woods. The other brigands reacted immediately. Two pistol shots rang out. Both hit Izaak, but neither had any effect. The bullets hit his body but did not pierce his skin—as if he were made of flint. The robbers gaped in astonishment and backed up. One reached out and seized Nelleke, putting a knife to her throat.

"Move one step and she dies," he said.

Somehow Nelleke knew his knife would not cut her. Power coursed through her body. She reached up with more speed than she could imagine herself capable, seized the man's arm, pulled it down, and spun around to face him. He slashed at her. His knife struck her throat but skidded off. Had it made sparks when it touched her flesh? The bandit gaped in fear. Nelleke swiped her hand at him. Her fingernails had turned to talons. The blow she gave tore the left side of his face away. Blooded spurted. The smell of it made her wild. She drew back her arm and punched him in the chest. Her hand penetrated his body, tearing through his sternum and into the heat of his insides. She grasped his heart and clenched her fingers, squeezing it. A low, guttering sound came from the brigand. He collapsed. The other two shrieked and fled into the forest.

Nelleke pulled her hand out. Squishy, wet with blood, it showed lurid in the dim light of the moon. Not waiting for a word from Izaak, she dove down, buried her face in the wound she had made, and began to suck the blood from his body.

As it flowed down her throat, she felt the maddening hunger ease. A satisfaction deep and rich as the sea filled her. She thought of nothing but the pulse of life restoring her. Clarity of mind returned. Sweet, indescribable bliss filled her. It took her ten minutes to desiccate his corpse. When she finished, turned, and stood up, Izaak was there.

"You know, there are neater ways to eat," he smiled.

She did not understand, but then saw that her face, arms, and the top part of the dress she wore were covered with blood. She felt it on her face and in her hair. Nelleke glanced down at the man Izaak had killed. A small, neat wound on the side of his neck revealed a trickle of red—nothing more. No trace of blood appeared on Izaak's clothing or face.

"There's a spring in the wood. You can wash there."

She glanced at the corpses.

"Do we just leave them?"

"They'll disappear," he said. "Creatures—magical creatures—will carry them away."

"What creatures?"

"We don't know. They appear—they look like giant bats—and take the corpses. Come on."

They plunged into the blackness of the thick, ancient wood. True to what she had surmised, she could see. The two of them wound their way past the huge trees, scared up deer and a bear, and at last came to the spring. Nelleke pulled off her garment and washed, also washing the blood-soaked dress she had been wearing. Immediately after washing she turned to Izaak and began to pull at his clothing.

Madness equal to the madness of the hunger she had satisfied passed over her. When his garments were off, she knelt in front of him, rubbing, licking, and sucking until he was ready. He put his arms around her, but she pushed him back to indicate what she wanted. He lay back. She climbed on top and worked her way down onto him. She began to move, her rhythm wild as the forest around her. Izaak put his arms around her as she writhed back and forth. He moved, just as wildly and with just as much strength, to match her movements, kissing her, gently biting her ears and cheeks, squeezing her so hard it almost drove the breath from her with each thrust. Orgasms exploded through her body like fireworks on celebration nights, one after the other. She shouted and shrieked, writhing on top of him, until she heard him groan and shout and felt him buckle and then release a warm stream of fluid into her. Peace and joy settled on her. She felt him relax as she did. For a long time they lay there, finally rolling onto their sides. She could see his smile.

"I wondered how it would be," he said. "Your love is so intense I thought it was going to kill me." He smiled. "Good thing we're both among the undead."

They lay in the forest. Through the towering trees, she could see the moon, the stars, and the silvery clouds. She thought of Anita. Somehow she would make it work. She would find a way and nothing would hinder her. Two deer walked by, stopped, gazed at them, and went on. When her garments were dry, they would return. She would be rested for when her child woke and needed to nurse.

VI

Nelleke followed Izaak to the city of London and moved in with him. He had a house in Southwerk (actually outside the city) not far from the Globe Theater. She settled into her new life among the undead.

Despair often seized her. She longed for the sun at first. But eventually she forgot daylight and began to loathe the very thought of the sun. A small coven existed in the city. Izaak was her primary mentor, but she met vampire women as well: Clarice, the leader of the coven, who had lived since the days of the ancient Romans; Tristana, a beautiful woman from the time of Henry IV, once mistress to Thomas Fitzalan, 6th Earl of Arundel (who was a character in Shakespeare's Richard II); Carmilla, who sought the love of women rather than the love of men; Amelie, a French girl who had fled her native country to escape religious persecution and who had a child. Nelleke was surprised at how few vampires were in the coven. "There aren't very many of us," Clarice told her. "In the city of London, we number only ten. This is good because if there were more of us people would notice the disappearances." *Disappearances* was one of the words she learned from the terminology vampires used: it meant the death of victims. The ten vampires in London, each feeding once a month, would kill sixty people a year. The program of finding blood had to be carried out not only with stealth but also with a workable strategy. Most found victims whose death would not be noticed: the homeless, beggars, the destitute, the wandering mad.

Nelleke followed Izaak's practice and tried to victimize only those she deemed immoral or vicious. She especially went after robbers and thieves, finding all her victims from among the ranks of those who stalked the night for nefarious purposes. The stalkers became the stalked, and when they disappeared few took notice.

She asked about the "bats" Izaak had mentioned.

"This is a mystery we don't understand," Tristana told her. "They are huge. I saw them only one time, and the sight frightened me so much I pissed myself. They materialize in the air, swoop down, take up the victims with the clawed hands on their wings, rise into the air, and then disappear. Some say they come from another world and feed on the corpses we leave behind. No one knows for certain. I will say, though, that they are a grace, wherever they dwell. If we left bodies behind, suspicion would arise. But the bats take the corpses away so we don't have to worry about concealing them."

Amelia helped her with Anita.

"How can I take her out at in the day?" Nelleke despaired. "A child needs sunlight. She can't live in darkness as I do!"

Tristana and Clarice, who both were wealthy, retained servant women who, they said, "understood" and would help care for her child. Several times a week, Martha Hogwood came to watch Anita. She would come before dawn and take the child out. Nelleke remained in her sun-proof house. When Anita grew older, Nelleke warned her she must not tell other children that her mother "never went out in the sun." Her child she seemed to understand the seriousness of the matter even in her early years. When she was ten, Nelleke told her the truth. But by that time she had already discerned it. She accepted the unimaginable and actually became friends with the vampires in the coven and with Desiree, Amelie's daughter. She also got help from Dorthea. She and Bernard had split up only a few years after they married. Dorthea had found employment with the English government and now lived in London. She watched Anita at night when Nelleke went out to play music—or to hunt.

As her child grew and as the years passed, Nelleke learned to navigate the intricacies of living as one of the undying. She found ways to socialize and mix with the living. She made connections with local musicians and, through one group who often performed music for drama productions, with writers and actors around London, though she maintained caution.

Nelleke visited Arabella on occasion. One night in the forest, Arabella taught her how to transform to a mist.—a thing Nelleke knew the undying could do but had been warned it was tricky and dangerous and not to be attempted without the help of teacher.

"It's difficult," Arabella said the night she agreed to mentor Nelleke through the transformation. "You must concentrate. If you don't keep your mind focused on what you're doing, you could dissipate and die. You must also focus because none of your human senses will function, though you'll have other sorts of perception. If you take the form of a mist, it will also temporarily befuddle your enemies."

"How? Will it take the breath from them?"

"Yes, though it will not kill them. It will only temporarily disable them. Transforming to a mist is a useful tool. But you must be willing to take the time to learn how to do it."

After several days and a score of failed attempts, Nelleke managed to transform herself to a dark mist; and she learned how to control her form and navigate when she took that form. And the first time she did so successfully, she found herself standing in the middle of the forest naked as the day she was born.

"Unlike when you change into a bat," Arabella smiled, "your clothes don't transform with you. You have a very beautiful body, Nelleke. Come on, let's go to the house and get something for you to wear."

Changing into a bat proved a great deal easier.

And the years flowed on.

Nelleke practiced her lute music to while away the hours when she stayed up in the day to be with Anita in the sanctuary of her sunproofed house. Clarice, who had a few connections among the nobility, and who considered it her duty to help her vampire confederates, mentioned Nelleke's ability to some of her contacts and she found herself invited to play music at dinners and dances. Once or twice she played, blindfolded, as philandering Elizabethan nobles bedded whores and mistresses and wanted music in the background (and was paid handsomely for it). She began to get a reputation as a musician. "I have a child and can only perform at night," she told people. When people asked about Anita's father, she said she was a widow.

Anita would eventually marry an actor and begin to appear on stage in clandestine productions where women were allowed on stage. Nelleke and Izaak drifted apart and she began to frequent the social functions of the middle-ranking nobility in London as a lutenist and as a woman who was available if the price was right. To reduce the number of men who might approach her, she charged an exorbitant amount of money for her favors. Becoming a vampire had released a massive surge of sexual energy and desire into her body and mind, and she did not mind occasionally engaging in prostitution. Her wealth increased with the passing of time.

She met John Bull at a concert/reception in England in 1610.

The talk and gossip that night centered on the disappearance of Lady Lytton. No one had seen in her in over a day, people said. Servants had found blood on her bed, it was whispered, and several people at the reception thought she might have been abducted or murdered and her corpse carried off.

Nelleke knew where the body had gone. No one in the room, she reflected, would ever imagine what had really happened. The era was one of growing rationalism, and educated, progressive people never allowed themselves to indulge in what they considered to be ancient superstitions.

"Perhaps gypsies," Leticia, a woman from a prominent home, said as a group of revelers, Nelleke included, stood about and drank wine.

"How could gypsies have gotten in the house and not been noticed?" Waller, a local politician, scoffed. "She lived on the third floor. They would have to have scaled the walls, and we know gypsies are not ingenuous enough to that."

"They're deceptive," Ardith, an older woman, said.

Waller snorted. "They're the off-scouring of creation, and common thieves and kidnappers. I'd rather say one of the servants."

"Nothing was stolen, and Lady Lytton was kind to her servants. None have absconded." Leticia turned to Nelleke.

"What do you think, my dear?" she asked, turning to Nelleke.

"I have no idea what might have happened to her," Nelleke answered, "though I grieve to know she is missing—and probably lost to us. She often had me play for her. Music seemed to ward off her frequent headaches."

Nelleke had played the lute for Lady Lytton on several occasions. She had also listened for anything her Ladyship had said concerning persecution of Jews and Protestants. As she raised a glass of Madeira to her lips, a servant appeared and announced the concert would begin. She followed the knot of people into the hall where the concert was to be held. She found a seat near the front. She wanted to be where John Bull would see her.

Waller took his place on one side, Carmilla on the other.

Bull walked out on stage. He was tall, trim, dressed in formal black, his pointed beard as dark as the outfit he had on—a black silk doublet with black hose and shoes, though the shoes had silver buckles. He bowed to the applause that greeted him and took his seat at the keyboard. Nelleke relaxed. He positioned himself, lifted his hands, paused for a long dramatic moment, and then began.

Nelleke felt the music engulf her. She was close enough to feel the vibration of the harpsichord as well as hear the notes, and she marveled at his fluidity, the intricacy of his composition, and the precision of his execution. His musical composition fell within the limits of traditional keyboard technique yet pushed toward something more radical, unorthodox, and (she mused) dangerous. Hearing radical, unorthodox music made her think of her own life and how the respectable people sitting all around her would be horrified if they knew she stalked the streets of London at night hunting for human blood.

Bull's fingers flew over the keys. A cascade of notes enveloped the audience. Her senses and reactions had heightened because she had drunk blood only a few hours ago. The music seemed to go down into her soul, to the root of her body, into her blood and into her flesh. The sensual rhythm made her secret parts quiver and her heart beat faster. She probably wouldn't arrange anything with Bull tonight, though she wanted to put her arms around him, wrap her legs around him, and move to his rhythm, to the music and beat of his body. He would think she was too fast if she tried that.

The one who had satisfied her hunger for blood was the missing Lady Lytton. Nelleke had selected her because she found out from Dorthea that Lady Lytton was an informer for the French government and had revealed the identity of several French Protestants who had not known her loyalties, confided in her thinking she was a coreligionist, and ended up tortured or killed as a result of her treachery.

She thought back, one part of her mind enjoying the harpsichord concert, one part remembering. She came to the estate where the Lady lived. In the darkness behind her lavish dwelling, Nelleke transformed to a bat. Knowing the windows would be open against the heat, she flittered upward, sailed through the casement, and resumed her human shape. Lady Lytton slumbered. Nelleke scanned the room. No servants about; very often, noble women had servants sleep in their bed chambers, sometimes in their beds. The room resonated silence. Nelleke went about her business, used the talons that replaced her fingernails when she hunted to slash open Lady Lytton's throat quickly and then stretched out beside her on the plush mattress and began slurping her blood. A cool breeze blew. Hunger had made her weak. As she drank, she felt her strength return. The blood poured down her throat, a surge of life, a taste of ecstasy. She sucked the corpse dry, rose, and went to the open window.

Below her, the street lay deserted. The houses around the estate stood dark. She let herself transform to a bat and flew into the forest where she changed shape again, marveling that her clothes transformed along with her body, and mounted the horse she had tethered there. Avoiding busy places, she rode home, encountering no one. Nelleke had found her way to the sun-proof apartment and closed the windows long before dawn lit up the sky. No one would find the body. The predatory creatures who followed vampires and carried off the remains of those they killed would neatly dispose of Lady Lytton's corpse.

Her mind returned to the concert as Bull finished the

first piece in his recital. As applause filled the room, Nelleke remembered what Dorthea, who was sitting just behind her, had told her the Archbishop of Canterbury said of Bull: *the man hath more music than honesty and is as famous for marring virginity as he is for fingering of organs and virginals.* She and Dorthea had enjoyed a long, unwholesome laugh over the sentence, speculating on whether or not the Archbishop knew he was punning.

"Where did you get that note?" Nelleke had asked.

"The priest who is his secretary for correspondence—and who used to lay me now and then—showed it me."

Dorthea, pale and slender, had an innocent look about her but, after splitting with Bernard, had slept her way into the upper ranks of British society in London and amid the recusants in Oxford. She infiltrated Roman Catholic enclaves within the land of England, supplied the government with information on British citizens who secretly maintain their Catholic faith and smuggled priests and Catholic radicals across the channel (hence her connection with the Archbishop). Nelleke turned her attention to Bull as he sat at the keyboard. He was getting along in years, but still looked as virile as his name suggested. He could finger her organs all he wanted, she smiled.

After performing three pieces, Bull rose, took a bow, and stepped down from the podium. Nelleke and Carmilla went back to the main rooms for more wine before dinner. In no time, Sir Robert Wolfe, who had designs on Nelleke, joined them. Bull was with him. Using her diplomatic and manipulative skills, she managed to leave Sir Robert with Carmilla and get in a secluded corner alone with Bull.

She had worn a burgundy gown with a low neckline that showed some cleavage, a small ruff, and a winged collar. She liked the way the tight sleeves showed off her slender arms. She hoped Bull like it as well.

"Your music is marvelous," she told him.

"I'm told *you're* quite a capable musician," he replied.

"I'm a player, not a composer."

"You can't have the second without the first. I'm told you play as well as any man."

She smiled coyly. "I don't know if that is a compliment or not." She added, "I've had quite a few years to practice."

A servant emerged and announced that dinner was served.

"Lord James said I could invite a guest of my choosing to dine at our table," Bull said. "He is keeping a place for whomever I choose. Would you care to join us?"

"I would be delighted," Nelleke beamed, in fact delighted that her stratagems had succeeded.

As they walked to the dining room she noticed that Sir Robert had Carmilla cornered and was inviting her to sit with him. Since she was unaccompanied, she would have no choice but to accept his invitation. She wouldn't like that, Nelleke reflected as she took Bull's arm and he led her into the dining hall.

VII

The next night, a knock came to Nelleke's door. She spied through the peephole. It was Carmilla. She kissed her friend and poured wine for her.

"So how was the party?"

"Do you even have to ask? I got pushed into a corner with Sir Robert. I ended up going home with him. I barely got out of his bed and got away before the sun came up."

Nelleke laughed. "I know you've been between the sheets with men quite a few times."

"I have, but I don't like it. And anyway, I met a girl yesterday and she's moving in with me."

"Anyone I know?" Nelleke knew all the vampire women in London and could not think of any of them who shared Carmilla's passions.

"She's a peasant girl who came to London to make her fortune—a mortal. Her name is Kimberly."

"You're taking up with a mortal?"

"Yes, I am."

"Do you really think you should do that?"

"Why not? You can't tell me you've never got it on with a moral, Nelleke. You have to do that for appearance's sake if for no other reason."

Nelleke blushed. "Well, yes, but you said she's a peasant girl. That isn't good. Peasants believe in us. The Lords and Ladies think we're a curious myth and don't question our not going out in the daylight because they stay up all night and sleep through most of the day. You're asking for trouble."

"If trouble comes, I'll deal with it."

"I hope you can. How much have you told her?"

"I said I am being pursued by a rich countess and can only go out at night."

"Do you think she'll believe that? Countesses who run after other women do what I just said: they stay up half the night and sleep till three in the afternoon. It will take that girl about a week to figure out why you don't leave your apartment during the day."

"I don't believe that and I don't want to talk about it. How did your dinner with John Bull go?"

"It went well. I'm visiting him at Oxford in a few days. I have an important engagement next week. I'm playing for the Queen."

"You're playing for the Queen? How did you rate that?"

"Bull arranged it. He has some clout in the palace."

"You're faulting me for taking a mortal as my lover. How about you? And what are you going to do if the Queen invites you to breakfast—or to one of her outdoor gatherings? For that matter, what are you going to tell Bull if he invites you out during the day?"

"I'll feign illness. Her Majesty is not feeling well and doesn't go outside her chambers much nowadays. She more or less lives in a dark room. She will be gone in a few months. And I plan to make certain I don't tell Bull about my real identity."

"I'm not planning to tell Kimberly about mine. You're the one who had better be careful, Nelleke."

Both of them wanted to change the subject. Nelleke poured wine for them and they sat and drank. After a long silence, Carmilla asked, "How is Anita doing? She's been married how many years now?"

"Four years. She has two children and is doing quite

well."

"Do you see Izaak?"

"I see him from time to time. I'm finding quite a few attractive vampire men in London."

"There are a lot of those here," Carmilla said glumly. "Unfortunately, not a lot of women who would want to be around me seem to live in the city."

Nelleke cooked a meal for them. They dined and gossiped.

"The man Anita married—is his name Giles?"

"Giles Gilbert. He's an actor."

"What troupe?"

"The Lord Chamberlin's men."

"I might have seen him perform."

Nelleke looked at her. "You went to a play? How did you manage that?"

Plays were mostly performed during the day in the open air.

"The Chamberlain's men did a performance for Lord Cecil. It was at night in a room lit with torches. Sir Robert invited me. The play was long, but parts of it caught my attention."

"What was the play called?"

"I can't remember. It's about two lovers whose families are fighting."

"*Romeo and Juliet*. Giles has the lead in that play."

"That was Giles?"

Nelleke didn't answer. She sat back in her chair. "I wonder if the Earl would let me into a performance."

"If you're willing to share the couch with him, of course he will."

Nelleke was quite willing to do as much. She resolved to contact him as soon as possible. She wanted to see Giles act. This might be her only opportunity.

They finished eating. "Be careful, Carmilla," Nelleke

warned as her friend got ready to leave. "That human girl will cause you trouble. Don't let love run you fool-headed."

Carmilla left. Nelleke rested, read, and then went out into the night. She transformed to a bat and flew high into the murky sky above London. She had not drank blood in a month. It was time to find some. One of the things that amazed her after she crossed into the world of vampire was that she still ate regular food. It seemed almost as if she existed as two creatures. Of course, as a vampire, she would live forever and not age. She could not have children and had ceased to menstruate. But everything else was the same. She breathed, felt her heart beat, felt pain, got cuts and bruises, ate and tasted food, eliminated waste, and had to bathe and shave her legs and under her arms. Other than not being able to go into the sunlight, she still felt mostly human. It was only when she hunted or found herself in danger that her vampire powers took over.

She flew to a place she had found to be a reliable hunting ground, crossed the stone bridge that bore houses and taverns, descended to the shoreline of Thames, and, using her ability to see in the dark, moved silently along the docks and streets, hoping to find someone suitable. Like Izaak, who had taught her the ways of the undead, she did not prey upon the innocent and good but found victims who did harm. After an hour of stealth, her ears picked up the sound of a woman whimpering and the muffled voices of men. She hurried around a corner and found what she had hoped to find. A burly man in a ragged cloak had two fashionably dressed Londoners at knifepoint and was demanding their money. She came up behind him and deliberately made a noise. He turned. Nelleke shouted "Flee!" to the people standing on the other side of the robber. He gave them a menacing glance and turned back to Nelleke.

"You stupid little harlot," he said. "Shut your mouth or

I'll kill you and toss your body into the Thames."

Just then the people he had meant to rob ran down a darkened side street.

It was too dark for him to notice her fangs or the talons on her fingers. When she rushed at him, he swung his knife. It hit her on the side of the head, but by then Nelleke's vampire spirit had taken control and, besides the fangs and talons, had made her skin like iron. His blade broke. For only a moment she saw the terror and disbelief in his expression. She swung her hand and struck him in the same place he had hit her. He crumpled into a heap.

As with predatory cats, vampires preferred to kill by hitting their victims and breaking their neck or slashing their throats open with talons. They rarely used their fangs to kill people; rather, they used them to rip open and enlarge the wounds they made with their talons or, if they broke the person's neck, to open veins and arteries. With the superhuman strength now available to her, she picked the robber up and carried him to the verge of the Thames, where she opened his throat and sucked the blood from his body.

She felt herself revive. Power coursed through her. The lethargy that had gripped her over the past week faded as she fed. He was a big man with lots of blood—just what she needed. After she had drained him, Nelleke kicked his body into the Thames. *High irony*, she thought as she transformed to a bat and sailed through a sky heavy with smoke from torches and lamps.

A week after finding her victim, Nelleke went to the appointment John Bull had arranged for her at the palace of the Queen of England shortly after darkness fell. Torches illuminated the gates. The Beefeaters, with their red uniforms and hauberks, stood three deep in two ranks at the heavy iron and wood entrance to the palace. One of the Queen's men greeted her and told her to come inside. She glanced around, marveling at the opulence of the residence. Polished marble floors reflected the light from torches hung on the walls. Tapestries and paintings lined the corridors leading to the room where she received supplicants and met with potential employees. Arched ceilings covered with gold leaf rose above Nelleke as she walked along. Servants dressed in red, blue, and purple livery scurried about bearing vessels that looked like they might be made of gold. Deep-colored wainscoting rose from the floor halfway up to where the murals and portraits told their mute stories.

Two more servants joined them, then another two, and escorted her to the Queen's chambers. They stopped before the door. Nelleke gave her lute to a lower-ranking maidservant.

Two Beefeaters opened the doors. As instructed, Nelleke knelt before the Queen and bowed her head. Elizabeth would not acknowledge her; a musician did not rate a word from a monarch. Nelleke maintained her bowed position until a serving woman handed her the lute, saying the Queen desired to hear her play. She then rose, walked to the chair, gave another small bow before she sat (she had to have special permission to sit in the presence of the Queen). Nelleke had paid to have her hair curled into ringlets and bought a dress embroidered with gold and yellow thread. She took the lute, did a quick tuning, and began to play.

Those managing the performance had let her decide which pieces she would play. She had chosen a tune by John Johnson, "Passing Measure Galliard," and "Packington's Pound," a popular tune. Bull had told her Johnson had written a marvelous piece of music but was too much of a dolt to perform it before the Queen. He also said Elizabeth liked "Packington's Pound," which she often heard sung in the streets, but no one would play it for her because the common people sung the song.

As Nelleke played, her anxieties about making a mistake dropped away and she began to play with energy as her long fingers moved; she crossed into the creative territory where musicians took risks and pushed their limits. Her fingers flew over the fretboard; her right hand plucked the strings with power and alacrity.

No one whispered as she played. The silence told her the Queen was enjoying her performance and no one dared speak lest they spoil her enjoyment. "If she doesn't like what you're doing, she'll start talking to the people attending her," Bull had told her. "Everyone in the room will start chatting and whispering and you will barely be able to hear yourself play." The silence meant she had made a good impression.

After the two pieces she had selected from other sources, Nelleke performed one of her own compositions. The inspiration for it had come from the folk tunes she had played in the Netherlands as a girl. Music sometimes found its way across the channel, but these songs were too obscure, too local, she thought, for anyone over here to know them. English composers came to the Netherlands, but they seldom paid attention to music the common people sang. She began the tune, not letting herself think the Queen might not like her composition. She played with confidence and, not fearful of failure, with verve.

When she finished, a silent pause came. She heard faint clapping. In a moment, the room filled with applause. The Queen had applauded and everyone else had followed suit. Nelleke stood and bowed. One of the men who stood near the queen came to her.

"Her Majesty would speak with you," he said.

Nelleke's heart began to beat more quickly. Leaving her lute in the hands of the serving women, she approached the throne. Her legs shook and she felt lightheaded. She had to be careful to suppress her vampire energies, which often emerged when she felt anxiety. Once she saw the golden shoes Elizabeth wore, she stood still. The Queen touched her. A jolt of fear and amazement ran through her. A very faint gasp went through the room—the people quietly reacting to seeing the Queen of England touch a commoner. Again, she fought down her fear. If she revealed her vampire self, it would mean her destruction. Fangs and talons would not do here. She fought for self-control.

"Arise," Elizabeth side. "Look up at me."

Nelleke lifted her eyes. Several people had told her that Elizabeth was ugly. Nelleke saw that the Queen wore a thick layer of white greasepaint makeup in an apparent effort to try to cover up her lack of beauty. Her hair shone a vivid red-orange. Nelleke thought that rather than being ugly she looked old, weary, and ill. She could see some of the Queen's former beauty. Traces of it remained.

"You play well, young woman."

"Thank you, my Queen. Your praise is the greatest reward I may know."

A faint smile came on Elizabeth's lips. "That last piece—I don't think I've heard it."

"My own composition, Your Majesty. I hope it pleased you."

"You will play for me tomorrow when the sun stands at three. I am ill. I sleep at that particular time of day. Music helps me fall asleep."

Nelleke felt a surge of fear, but she smiled. "I will be privileged to do so, my Queen."

Elizabeth nodded at one of the four men dressed in formal black who stood about her. He gave Nelleke a bag of coins. She bowed low and walked backwards to where the serving woman waited with her lute. When she got back to her apartment, she opened the bag and found it full of gold florins.

VIII

Though pleased with the money, she wondered how she would manage to get safely to the palace in daylight. Eventually, though, she managed to work out a system. The Queen most often wanted her to play at night in her bedchamber so she could go to sleep more easily. On rare occasions when Nelleke was commanded to play in the day, she made arrangements to stay in one of guest rooms, creating various reasons for her wanting stay there; the officials, not wanting to antagonize someone the Queen favored, always agreed to her request for lodging.

A few weeks later, she was practicing for an upcoming performance when someone pounded at her door. It was Amelie, a French vampire girl who had escaped the Inquisition and fled to England. Babbling in French, which Nelleke spoke, she said Carmilla had been arrested and imprisoned. The Council of Vampires in London had convened to consider a response to Carmilla's capture. Clarice, the head of the Council, had ordered everyone to attend. She had sent Amelie to notify Nelleke.

They hurried through the dark streets to the house where the Council had assembled. Once inside, she and Amelie entered a large room lit by candles. Nelleke saw the entire coven of London—all of the vampires she knew-- sitting at a table in the center of the room. She and Amelie bowed to Clarice, who sat at the head of the table. Since the others had already given their opinions, Nelleke got to speak at once.

We've got to set her free," she said.

"Why?" Desford, one of the middle-ranking vampires in the coven, demanded. "She brought this on herself."

"We can't abandon her. We can't let her die."

"Why can't we? And why are you so concerned with her safety?"

"Because she is my friend and I love her. If she took up with a mortal woman, it's because she is so lonely. And that isn't forbidden, is it? I have lovers who are mortal. I know some of you here in this room do this as well."

"It's one thing to have a mortal lover. It's another to give away your identity as one of the undying," Desford answered.

"Maybe she didn't use as much caution as one needs to use in such matters," Nelleke replied, "but we can't abandon one of our own."

The Council members did not look convinced.

"Where is she being held?" Tristana asked.

"In the Tower."

"Why hasn't she transformed?" Desford asked. "She could change to a bat, fly up to the top of her cell, stay there until they opened the door, and then fly through a window. I don't see how they can keep her prisoner."

"If they're torturing her, she would be in too much pain to transform," Amelie said.

"But it doesn't make sense," Tristana observed. "She would have had opportunity to transform before they started to torture her, if that is what they're doing. And if she's still alive, it means they're keeping her out of the sunlight. They know she's one of us. How would that be?"

"The question we need to deal with first," Izaak said, "is how we can get her out? If she breaks under torture and reveals our identities, we're all in trouble. We need to rescue her, or it may mean the end of the coven."

"All the cells in the Tower have windows," Clarice put in. "I know this because in my early days I had occasion to visit prisoners I knew who were confined there. I don't understand why she hasn't died from that, since she has been imprisoned there in the daylight hours."

"If they know she's one of our kind, they might be keeping her in an inner chamber where the sunlight does not come. If the mortal girl who told them Carmilla is a vampire, and if they want to torture her, they would be careful not to expose her to the sun. And Izaak is right. They want to know about the coven. They want to hunt us down. We know Carmilla. She isn't brave. She'll tell them everything, including our identities. We must get her out of there."

The Council sat silent when they heard this. Finally, Desford spoke.

"Well, it might be prudent to make an attempt," he said. "Clarice, you're the senior member of the Council. Give us your judgment."

"Nelleke is correct. We need to free her. We can decide how to discipline Carmilla after she is freed. How can we do it?"

"As Desford noted, it won't be hard to get in," Brendan, a younger vampire, commented. "One of us can fly in. The trick will indeed be getting her out. Do you think she will be able to transform?"

"Carmilla isn't good at transforming," Nelleke said. "And she's afraid and weak."

Silence fell once more. Nelleke wondered how it would be if the government began a campaign against the coven. She could tell every mind in the room was occupied with the same worry.

"If I may speak," Amelie said. Everyone turned to her. Fair and lovely, she radiated beauty in the dark chamber where the Council had met. She went on in heavily accented

English. "Please you, my masters and mistresses," she said. "I know where one of the guards—one of the Beefeaters—lives. He lives near to me and I see him leaving at times in his red uniform. He is a young man and lives alone. If we can take his uniform, we might gain access to the prison."

The Council seemed to brighten at her words.

"If we can get her out of her cell and into the open air," Brendan said, "we might be able to get her away from there. It's worth the risk. If the king's agents find out who we are and where we live, we'll have to flee London and make lives elsewhere. They could disestablish the entire London coven." His eyes darkened. "And I think Carmilla has committed a serious crime that compels us to punish her appropriately."

Nelleke did not say anything, but she remembered what had happened to Eseld.

X

The tension from the meeting exhausted Nelleke. After several hours of sound sleep, she awoke with the sense that someone was in her house. Fearing that Carmilla had already been broken by torture to reveal information about the rest of them, she climbed out of bed and cautiously entered the kitchen. Relief flooded through her when she saw Izaak sitting at the table.

"You could have knocked," she said.

"I needed to get inside. It rained and I thought it was safe to go outside, but the storm stopped and the clouds were breaking." He glanced at her. "You sleep in a smock now?"

She came over and sat down across from him. "I always did at home. And now I don't have anyone in my bed to keep me warm."

"Do you miss home?"

"Of course I do. But"—she made a vague gesture. "What are you doing in London? I thought you had moved to Calais permanently."

He smiled sadly. Somehow their love had flickered and gone out. By the time Anita married they had drifted apart. Izaak had been with Dorthea for a while and, with her connections, began doing espionage for the British and Dutch government. Of late, he had lived with a vampire in Calais.

"How is Denyse?" Nelleke asked.

"I don't know."

She looked over at him. "So you've left her? You're leaving behind quite a string of abandoned lovers."

"It wasn't my choice."

"And now you're here."

"If you want to know the truth, Denyse left me for a Russian who leads the coven in St. Petersburg. I was unceremoniously discarded."

"I'm sorry.

"It was time. We were boring each other. I hear now and then from the Coven, and got news of this by a couple of our people I know who go back and forth from London to Calais. I want to help. My friends told me Desford wants to stake her. Even if you and the others manage to get her free from the Tower, she'll face execution because she's put the coven in danger. What she did was stupid. Why didn't you warn her?"

"Don't you think I did? She won't listen to me."

"Well, either way, it's over for her."

"We need to set her free and then we can talk about that."

"They tell me you've become a court musician."

"People talk too much. What time is it?" she asked.

"Seven. The sun's down."

Do you want breakfast?"

She cooked eggs and a rasher of bacon. They ate the food and drank ale. Nelleke noticed Izaak kept stealing glances at her. She had consorted with different men in the coven but had never found one she really liked. As if reading her thoughts, he reached over and took her hand.

"Do you think…"

"Don't say it. However you put it, it will sound trite. But yes."

"Desford said you were seeing Bertrand."

"I was," Nelleke said, taking a sip of ale. "He dumped me for Amelie—which I can fully understand. She's much prettier than I."

"Bertrand was alive when the Normans invaded. I'm not surprised he got it up for a pretty little French girl."

"Pretty isn't the right word. She's the most beautiful girl in England. She's sweet and I love her a lot." A tap came at the door.

Nelleke threw on a garment and answered. A boy in a servant's uniform carrying a lantern bowed and gave her a letter. She handed him a coin, and he scurried away.

"His livery was the uniform they wear at the palace. What's this all about?"

"It's about trouble, I imagine," Nelleke answered, breaking the wax on the letter. The seal of the Lord Chamberlain lay imprinted in the wax. Izaak watched. Nelleke broke off her reading.

"Just what I was afraid of. They want me to play during the daytime. This whole thing might get too difficult to manage. I might have to leave—damn it. I like it here."

"We'll see what we can do."

"We?"

Before Izaak could answer, another knock came at the door. This time whoever it was beat the pattern indicating a coven member had arrived. It was Bertrand.

"Izaak, hello. Someone told me you were back."

Bertrand and Izaak did not like each other. *The fact,* Nelleke mused, *that both of them have fucked me gives the whole situation an enjoyable bit of drama.*

Bertrand, who was not one for social amenities, immediately got down to business.

"Amelie and I managed to get the uniform. She didn't want to kill the Beefeater, kind soul that she is, so we made it look like a burglary. We have probably three hours before the young man wakes and reports the theft of his uniform.

We need to get moving. Izaak, are you in with us on this venture?"

"I'll do anything I can do to help."

Bertrand regarded him. "I think I know just the thing."

The three of them moved quickly. Izaak hurried off with Bertrand. Nelleke went outside, locked her house, and transformed.

She flew high into the air. The rain that came earlier in the day had washed down the smoke of a hundred thousand fires burning in hearths. Nelleke moved through the temporarily cleansed sky. Transformation still intrigued her. She could become a thing (mist) or a creature (a bat). In both forms, she was blind; when she turned to a mist, which was more difficult—she had only done so twice—she had no senses at all. In the body of a bat, she experienced "seeing" by the vibrations that came to her ears, the scents that entered her nostrils, the currents, heat and cold that touched her tiny body. She did not understand how she could assume the shape of a creature like this yet still have human thought and reason—just as she could not understand how her garments transformed just as her body did, but didn't transform with her when she became a mist. She rode the air currents and, sending out the high-pitched squeaks by which a bat navigates, knew when she neared the Tower. She flew around it, detected an opening, and swooped in.

She lit in an upper hall. Listening, she heard screaming and begging. Carmilla. Nelleke moved forward, keeping to the shadows in the corridor and came to the door from the chamber from which Carmilla's voice sounded—it had a choked, muffled quality. She wondered what they were dong to her.

"*For the love of mercy!*" Carmilla screamed madly.

Laughter followed, and men's voices. "Love of mercy? You murdering ghoul! Drinker of human blood! How much mercy have you shown to those upon whom you prey?"

Nelleke heard more scoffing guffaws and then a frantic plea followed by a metallic noise and more of Carmilla's screams. Nelleke steeled herself. She wanted to rush in and liberate her friend but checked herself. *Self-control*, she thought, and breathed in slowly to check her anger.

More noises, more sounds of rusty hinges, and Camilla's wailing died away to hysterical sobs. Nelleke heard a voice, quieter than before. She leaned closer to the door and listened. "Now, you whore of the Devil, listen for your own good. We've given you a taste of what we can do to you—and this is only the beginning. The Lord Chancellor will be here in a few hours to question you. If you don't answer him, you know what will happen." The sound of someone being repeatedly slapped and more of Camilla's pathetic begging and shouts of anguish followed. Nelleke heard the sound of heavy boots and transformed once more, fluttering to the lintel above the cell door and fastening there. Though she could not see them, she sensed a group of four men leaving the room. The last one out locked the door. The men laughed and joked as they made their way down the stairs.

She glided to the floor and changed her form. Carmilla's interrogators had not posted a guard. They had locked the door, though. Drawing on the strength available to her when she called up her vampire soul, Nelleke gripped the door handle and turned it. It did not budge. She pressed her lips together, reached deep into her spirit, felt her fangs grow and her body transform. The steel tongue of the lock snapped loudly. She stood still and listened. Hearing no one approach, she went inside.

Just past the door, Nelleke felt dizzy and nauseous. The floor seemed to move sideways. She almost fell. She saw Carmilla lying in a corner of the room in a pile of dirty straw. She wore a soiled smock. Trembling and crying, she lay there, limbs jerking, eyes wide and terrified. Nelleke saw blood running from her nose, eyes, fingers, and toes. In the center of the room stood a device made of two circular metal hoops. She shuddered with horror. The Scavenger's Daughter—a torture device that crushed the human body—one of cruelest machines ever designed by diabolical craftsmen.

Carmilla saw her. Her pale face registered hope. Her lips moved as they would to say Nelleke's name but no sound came out. Nelleke gaped and then fell. Her face was close to Carmilla's

"What's happening?" Nelleke asked, her voice thick and labored. "I can hardly walk or move."

"The jewel," Carmilla whispered, cocking her head to one side. "Magic."

Nelleke struggled to her feet and stumbled in the direction Carmilla had indicated. Ahead of her, a large emerald hung from a post by a gold chain. As Nelleke stared, it went out of focus. She extended her arm to seize it.

"No!" Carmilla said. "Don't touch it! It will kill you if you touch it."

Nelleke saw the jewel blur. She refocused her eyes.

"Box," Carmilla whispered. "Put it in the box underneath it."

She said *put it in the box* not as a sentence but as separate words given with much effort at long intervals. Sweat poured from Nelleke's body as she searched for what her friend indicated. Her eyes fell on a dark-colored box just below the jewel. She reached down for it but miscalculated and fell forward, hitting her chin on the table. With much effort, she got up and grasped the box with both hands. *Lead*, she thought. She lifted it. Even with the strength she acquired when controlled by her vampire self, she could barely lift the casque, small as it was. Nelleke fixed her will and moved the container upward.

Her ears popped. She felt her hair stand on end.

Sweat soaked the upper parts of her dress. Evil and anger flowed out of the green jewel—but, paradoxically, under it, sorrow, love, and longing. The anger dominated. It struck her in debilitating waves. She tried to align her soul with the other strain she felt in the magic affecting her: on the peace and beauty amid the anger and hatred that buffeted her. When she did this, the debilitating magic lessened. The lead container moved slowly upward. She heard the emerald strike on its bottom. Pain shot through her arms and radiated down to her feet. She felt as if someone was pulling her teeth out. Finally—it seemed like she had been standing there a thousand years—she brought the box level with the peg on which the jewel hung and shook it so the jewel fell in the casque. She snapped the box shut and set it on the table.

Nelleke felt herself jolt into bright, sharp sensibility. Vision clear, pain gone, nausea and dizziness fled away; she hurried over and knelt to be close to Carmilla.

Two streams of blood ran from Carilla's eyes like red tears and had dried on her nose and lips. Her fingers and toes had turned black from compressed blood. Droplets oozed from them. She had wet and soiled herself. Nelleke remembered, perhaps absurdly, how beautiful Carmilla's hands had been: white, with long, slender fingers, elegant in their motions. She snapped back to a determined mindset, leaned closer to her friend, and touched her gently.

"We're going to get you out," she said.

Unable to answer, Carmilla sobbed.

"Be still." She looked about. If things went according to plan, someone wearing the uniform Amelie had stolen would appear to take Carmilla out of the Tower. Despite her distress, Nelleke knew she needed to talk to Carmilla.

"Did you tell them anything—anything about the coven?"

She shook her head.

"I know you've been through horrors, but you need to answer me. Tell me what you told them."

"Nothing," she wept. "They only tortured me. They didn't ask me about the coven or anything else." She fell into a paroxysm of sobbing, managed to get control of herself, and said, "Nothing. I didn't tell them anything." Nelleke heard steps, ran to the door, and peeked out. A man in a red uniform and the distinctive black hat approached. He stood tall and wore his dark hair long. As she came closer, she gasped. Izaak. She gave him a cautious smile as he hurried toward her.

"Is she awake?"

Nelleke said she was.

"I told the guards at the door she had died and I needed to throw her body in the river."

Izaak went into the torture room. He flinched when he saw the Scavenger's Daughter but said nothing. Carmilla had managed to raise herself to a sitting position.

"Carmilla, you need to quiet yourself so you're not breathing and have no heartbeat."

This was something vampires could do. She nodded. He turned to Nelleke. "You can transform and fly out. I'll meet you at Bertrand's place."

"No," she shot back. She picked up the casque. "There's a talisman in here. It casts a powerful spell. That's how they were keeping Carmilla captive. We need to steal it so they can't use it against us."

"How will you get it out the door?"

She pondered a moment. "I have an idea."

The two of them descended the stairs to the main floor. The gate guards, who, like any good sentries, were suspicious of Izaak because they had not seen him before, stopped him. He held Carmilla in his arms. Pale, not breathing, she looked dead. *Of course,* Nelleke thought, *she was, technically.* They placed fingers in front of her nostrils and on her neck to check for pulse. They nodded.

"The Lord Chancellor isn't going to like this," one commented.

As he finished speaking Nelleke appeared. The guards immediately closed ranks, blocking the door. Izaak hesitated but went outside. He carried Carmilla to an alleyway where Clarice, Bertrand, and Desford waited. They had brought an oxcart. They laid Carmilla in the back and covered her with a blanket. Desford took the reins. The cart lumbered into the shadows.

Back at the Tower, Nelleke faced the guards.

"Who are you, woman, and how did you get in here?"

"Do I have to do the two of you as well? Belinda didn't tell me about you."

Belinda Carlyle operated a notorious brothel just a block from the Tower.

"Answer our question," one of the said.

"I was brought here," Nelleke answered, feigning annoyance, "to fuck the guards on duty tonight—the ones giving that succubus woman what she deserved. Belinda told me it would be four men. I've rolled with all of them. She didn't tell me about you two, but people make mistakes. If you want me, all right—that's why I'm here. Where can we lie?"

Both guards were religious. Suspicion made them wary. She didn't have on a low-cut, tight-fitting dress and her hair was not in long ringlets. She did not have on makeup. Her dress did not match that of the whores they saw in the streets going to and fro from their jobs. They also noted she spoke more articulately than the women the other Beefeaters occasionally brought here to ply their trade. Nelleke stood impatiently. "Well?" she finally said, tapping her foot. "Show me where to put my back and I'll get to work."

The ranking guard stepped aside. "Return to the whorehouse where you belong," he said. He caught sight of the box. "What's that?"

"It's my pay." She shook the box. The sound it made suggested coins or a jewel. If the container had been gold or silver, or if it had been encrusted with gems, the guards might have investigated further; but a lead box was proper for holding a whore's wages.

"Go on, you stupid little trull," he said, "before we take you to the magistrate and have you whipped through the streets for your harlotry. Begone!"

Clutching the box, Nelleke hurried past them. Knowing they were watching, she walked haughtily, wiggling her bottom as she went her way, finally turning into the alleyway where Izaak and Desford stood waiting. Nelleke nodded to the question in their eyes and the trio hurried through the night to the secluded house where the Council had once more gathered.

Carmilla lay in a bed chamber. She had recovered enough from the magic of the jewel that she had been able to heal herself from the effects of the physical torture she had been subjected to. Vampires were vulnerable to injury when their vampire spirit was not in full possession of their bodies, as had been the case when the jewel's magic had overcome Carmilla's super-human powers. Now that the spell had lifted, she could use her vampiric powers to heal herself. But the trauma of the magic and the horror she had experienced through the course of it had left her weak. Nelleke tapped on the doorpost and came into the room.

"Nelleke," she said. Emotion overwhelmed her. Nelleke touched her hair.

"Be quiet. You need to get your strength back."

She turned her gaze to Izaak, who smiled compassionately. After more words with Carmilla, Izaak and Nelleke went into the main room of the house. The Council had gathered. They sat around the lead casque. All looked up when the two of them entered. Nelleke bowed and took her place at the table. Clarice had elected to preside once again. A retiring, quiet (and beautiful) woman, she often allowed others to chair the coven's gatherings. Not tonight.

"Two things," she began. "First, speaking for the London coven, I express our thanks to all of those who risked themselves in the venture to free Carmilla. Desford, Bertrand, and Amelie—and, particularly, Nelleke and Izaak, who ventured into the Tower—our thanks and gratitude to all of you." She paused and continued. "And Nelleke, you endured the power of the charm the authorities used to drain Carmilla of her strength. We opened the casque just for a moment and felt its power. This confirmed what Bertrand and I suspected. It is the Emerald of Aldebaran."

A quiet shudder passed through the room; Nelleke did not understand the fear she saw on the faces of the various undead. Clarice noticed her puzzlement.

"Nelleke, you are young. This stone is an ancient talisman. It disables our kind. No one knows its origin, but by its use the vampires of northern England were decimated. But then the stone vanished. No one knows why, but it has not been seen for 500 years. Its appearance would be a source of fear, but you have secured it for us. You will be rewarded for this. We marvel that, given your youth, you were able to endure its malevolent energy."

"I don't know how, my lady," Nelleke replied. "The charm pulled my spirit out of my body. I could hardly move and barely see."

"We are in your debt. We can seal the stone away so it will never be a threat again. The Council will determine your reward for this bravery. For now, you may ask anything and it will be given to you. You have saved us from destruction."

Nelleke only bowed her head. Clarice went on.

"And now we must consider discipline for Carmilla—and discipline it will be. She must be punished for her foolishness, which might have meant our coven's destruction. I open this up to the opinions of those gathered here. I have received opinions from four of our kind who could not be her tonight. All condemned her to destruction."

"I can endorse that," Desford said. "I even wonder why we're considering this question. What she did was stupid and potentially destructive. She has forfeited her right to exist."

Silence followed. Everyone seemed in agreement with Desford. Nelleke knew she needed to speak up.

"I counsel mercy," she said. "Carmilla behaved inappropriately. I don't dispute that. But it was out of her loneliness and need to find a companion."

"She has admitted than when the girl questioned her, she told her she was a vampire. You pointed out, Nelleke, that you have had human lovers. So have I. But neither of us has revealed our true nature to them. *That* is the practice Carmilla violated. Perhaps it is not written down in our by-laws, but common sense dictates as much."

"It seems to me," Desford interjected, "that it would not be difficult for her to find a companion without doing something as idiotically dangerous as blabbing about your true identity—your identity as one of the undying—with a mortal."

The room fell silent once more. Nelleke saw that her favorable words had not swayed anyone.

"I only council mercy," she said. "What she did put all of us at risk. I know that. I could easily have died in the attempt to rescue her. But are we no better than the men who were abusing her? I heard the sound of her being tortured and beaten. They scoffed at her pleas and said she didn't deserve mercy because she was a ghoul and the Devil's whore. It is our opportunity to show her grace. The guards in the Tower had not only beaten and tortured Carmilla, but raped and sodomized her. I heard her cries of pain as they used the Scavenger's Daughter on her. And will we rescue her from that and then destroy her? I suggest she has learned wisdom—learned it in a most horrific manner. I'm sure the lesson will not be lost on her. We should spare her and show her the mercy the living said she did not deserve and was not capable of."

"Clarice has said you can have whatever you want, Nelleke," Desford put in. "Why don't you use that boon to ask for Carmilla's life?"

"I won't because that would be forcing the Council's hand. I will abide by whatever decision our coven reaches. Only remember she is one of our kind. She acted foolishly and suffered for her foolishness; and the Coven of London has benefitted from her transgression, serious though it might have been. We secured the jewel—a weapon the authorities would have turned on us whether Carmilla had been captured or not."

She glanced about her. The other vampires contemplated what she had said. Clarice turned to Izaak.

"Izaak, we're happy to see you again. You put yourself in danger as well. Do you have anything to add?"

"Among my people, if a man fails and ruins himself, the community will come to his aid so he doesn't sink into penury. But only twice. If his improvident behavior causes him to fall in debt a third time, the community has no obligation to help him out. He has been rescued two times. Extending such a favor to three would be an insult to generosity and good will. Maybe, given the danger in which we constantly live, two opportunities for righting a person's wrongdoing would be one too many; but one opportunity to show mercy would not be excessive."

Again, silence. The coven members thought through what they had heard. After a long pause, Clarice went around the circle of twelve. Bertrand would give the first opinion.

Nelleke held her breath. Bertrand harbored humane notions, but he could be pragmatic and stern. After a long silence, he spoke.

"I suppose," he sighed, "she might live. We should show mercy to our own. I would suggest exile, though. We cannot allow someone who almost got all of us killed to live among us."

As the coven members spoke, Nelleke saw that her plea and Izaak's suggestion had won the day—though all members of the Council agreed that Carmilla should be exiled.

"I guess I could agree to that," Desford said grumpily when his turn came, "but only on the condition that I get to kick her ass when she boards the ship for France."

A small laugh ran around the circle, breaking the tension. Desford smiled. The mood in the room lightened.

"I think, then, we are in agreement," Clarice concluded. "Carmilla will leave the Isle of Britain. Other than that, no penalties will be exacted—expect for a possible kick in the rump when she embarks."

This time the group laughed loudly. A couple of the vampires applauded.

"Very well. The Council is adjourned. Nelleke, come with me. I want you to be there when I inform Carmilla of our decision."

The meeting broke up. The vampires went their separate ways. Nelleke followed Clarice into the room where Carmilla rested. She tried to sit up when Clarice entered. The woman gently touched her shoulder.

"No. you don't need to get up." Nelleke saw the fear in her friend's eyes. "We reached a decision, Carmilla, and you're not going to be destroyed. However, we are commanding you to leave London and Albion forever. We're sending you to France."

Now and then Clarice still used the old Roman name,

Albion, for England.

"You are merciful, my lady," Carmilla said, eyes full of tears.

"Carmilla, we love you. You behaved foolishly. I hope the things you went through taught you a lesson—though no one from among the dead or the living should endure what you endured. Still, take the lesson to the serious part of your soul. And you need to thank Nelleke. She and Izaak spoke in your favor. Had they not, I'm not certain the Council's decision would have been so auspicious for you, child."

Carmilla nodded. When she blinked, two big tears ran down her cheeks. Clarice left. Nelleke knelt by the bedside. Carmilla tried to speak but could not. Nelleke held her hand as she cried. After a while, she managed to say, "Thank you."

"It's nothing anyone would not do for a friend."

This made Carmilla sob for several more minutes. She finally quieted down. Nelleke gave her a cloth to dry her eyes.

"I am in your debt forever," she said.

"Don't think of it. Are you feeling better?"

"I managed to walk around the room a couple of times. I'm gathering strength. I'll have to have blood before I can fully recover, but I'll feel up to hunting later tonight."

"Good. If you need anything before you go, let me know."

Outside, the night watchman called the hour. Two. Nelleke knew she needed to get back to her house. Izaak would stay with her tonight. Maybe they could mend their relationship. She kissed Carmilla, pulled the quilt up around her shoulders, walked through the quiet house, and stepped out into the dark streets of London to her home just beyond the wealthy dwellings in Covent Garden.

XI

Nelleke and Dorthea felt the carriage that was taking them to the gathering jolt to a halt. The two of them climbed out and approached the gate of Wriothesley, Earl of South Hampton's estate. The servants and guard looked at the invitation John Bull had given Nelleke. He had to perform a concert that night and could not attend the play. "Besides," he had quipped when she left his house that day, "I've already seen the play." The servants admitted the two women and gave them an escort down the torch-lined path that led to the formidable house.

They came into the brightly lit entry hall. Servants wearing black uniforms embroidered with gold took their cloaks. Women in spangled gowns with elaborately piled-up hair and men wearing velvet jackets, doublets, hose, and highly polished shoes stood in knots or in pairs drinking and talking. Nelleke concealed a smile at how the plumes on the hats of the men bobbled as they bent their heads to listen someone standing near them. A consort of musicians with viols, lutes, and recorders played on a stage in one corner of the room. Servants in livery poured drinks and dispensed pastries. The two women sipped dark red glasses of madeira, savoring the rich, full taste. Nelleke spotted Richard Burbage and, next to him, William Shakespeare.

He had dark skin—so dark he might be an Italian or a Sephardic Jew from Palestine or Morocco. His hair, receding in front, hung in coal black locks around his ears. He wore a scruffy black beard and was dressed in a burgundy doublet with dark blue hose. Sipping a glass of wine, he smiled and spoke with easy confidence to Burbage, a handsome man who had played leads in Marlowe's and Kyd's plays and now did the leads in Shakespeare's works. She had seen him in Beaumont and Fletcher's *Philomela* performed, like this production, at night in a private home. Shakespeare, who had been an actor and still appeared on stage from time to time, had played a part. This is how she had recognized him.

"Is that the author of the play?" Dorthea asked.

Nelleke nodded. She finished her cake, went over to a bowl set up on one of the tables, and dipped her fingers to get rid of the stickiness. She wanted to talk to Shakespeare but knew it would be too forward for a lady not accompanied by a man to initiate a conversation. A bell rang announcing the play would begin. She and Dorthea found seats near the front. Two actors walked on stage. A moment later, a fight ensued between rival families. The rush of action pulled Nelleke in at once. As the play continued, though, its language caught her imagination, drawing her deep into the plot. She listened to the main character, played by her son-in-law, speak out a short soliloquy.

> *But soft! What light through yonder window breaks?*
> *It is the east, and Juliet is the sun.*
> *Arise, fair sun, and kill the envious moon,*
> *Who is already pale with grief,*
> *That thou her maid art far more fair then she...*

She blenched slightly, feeling her own loneliness, her longing for Izaak and her chagrin at him, but very quickly those feelings passed as the drama caught her up in its unfolding. When Romeo and Tybalt fought their duel, Nelleke was biting her knuckles. Dorthea touched her and, getting her attention, told her with an amused glance to lighten up. She smiled and nodded. They sat through to the end. Hearing the last words of the play, seeing the parents and citizens of Verona mourn the young people who had died, tears came to her eyes. The audience rose, applauded, and, after bows had ended, began to filter out of the room.

A young man approached them and bowed. "Dorthea," he smiled took her hand and kissed it. She returned the smile and introduced him to Nelleke. Dorthea had told Nelleke about him. He was a recusant, an Englishman who had refused to join the Anglican Church and remained a Roman Catholic. He also worked actively to smuggle priests and Catholic literature into the country. Dorthea had been collecting condemning evidence on him. She had told Nelleke just last week that he would be arrested in no time, tortured for information, and then hanged—probably within the month.

"There will be fireworks later," he said, "would you ladies care to join me on the lawn?" He noticed the tears in Nelleke's eyes.

"You're crying," he observed, slightly amused.

"The play moved me a great deal."

He laughed. "It wasn't bad, though I'm not sure we should be watching a work for stage written by a Warwickshire peasant. It is amazing he can write that well. He's never been to university, I hear."

"As if that means anything," Dorthea returned. "De Vere, the Earl of Oxford, performed one of his plays here." Nelleke and the young man looked at her, expecting more. "It put me to sleep," she said. "It was the most garbled, pointless fiction I've ever endured."

At that moment, Giles, her son-in-law, approached. Dorthea went with the doomed young man. Nelleke embraced him.

"Is Anita here tonight?" she asked.

"No. If I had known you were going to be here, I would have had her come along."

"I need to visit you two. I simply can't find the time with all that's been going on."

"She misses you."

"I'll be certain to get over."

Giles knew she was a vampire. He would be the only person in the room besides Dorthea who knew this.

"Will you introduce me to Master Shakespeare?"

At that moment, he walked on to stage. Giles flagged him down and introduced them.

"Your daughter is a charming woman," Shakespeare told her. "We think a great deal of her."

"I cherish her. Of course I would. She is my only child."

And, she thought, the only child she would ever have now that she had entered the world of the undying.

"You hardly look old enough to be her mother. I would say you were her sister if I knew no better."

"I gave birth to her at a young age. And people do tell me I have aged well."

"Better than anyone I know. But that's no matter. I'm charmed to meet you."

"I was charmed by your play," she said, a little unsettled that he had noticed how young she looked. "It was a marvelous work of art."

"Thank you. We're taking it on tour soon. Giles here will have the lead again." Giles went off to talk to some nobility. Nelleke and Shakespeare enjoyed a second glass of wine.

"You have an accent, like I do, although it doesn't sound like mine," he observed. "We speak with more of a brogue in Warwickshire. You?"

"I come from the Low Countries." She told him how she had learned English as a child.

"You speak it much better than Dorthea."

"You know Dorthea?"

"I have connections with the Bassano family. I've seen her there. I saw you once there as well. You were playing with the family consort."

Nelleke remembered. One of the family members who played lute had fallen ill. Izaak recruited Nelleke to fill in for him. The hall had been crowded. Nelleke had never seen the music until she sat down to perform and gave her focus totally to the notes, sight-reading, listening to the other musicians, her eyes riveted to the score the entire time. No wonder she had not noticed Shakespeare in the crowd.

"At first I thought you were Amelia."

Amelia Bassano was one of the family of musicians who had come from Italy to play for King Henry VIII and had established themselves as court musicians, serving through the reigns of Henry, Edward, Mary, and, now Elizabeth. They had created a dynasty, passing positions among the King's players on to their sons. They made and repaired instruments. They were also secret Jews.

"I kept my eyes on the score that night," Nelleke responded. "I don't mind being compared to Amelia, though. She's quite lovely."

Shakespeare laughed. "I very much agree. She is a dark lady, like you. The men of England seem to prefer the fair. If your skin is light, your eyes blue or green, and your hair golden, you are an object of worship. Poets will shower praise on you. Those with darker hair and eyes seem to have been demoted and pushed down the scale of beauty toward a footman's pittance."

She laughed.

"Would you like to go out on the lawn? The Earl has paid sumptuously for fireworks, I hear, and they should be enjoyable."

Nelleke remembered Shakespeare was married. Normally this would not have bothered her in the least, but they were in a public place. People gossiped and looked for material for scandal—and if you were a vampire you could not afford to be noticed too much. Shakespeare saw the look on her face and smiled.

"You must remember," he said, "these are the nobility. They will take no notice of us. Even if they did censure me for being with you, they would feel it below their dignity to take the matter up. To them, we're cattle, peasants, people who exist to serve and please them. Come along."

And with that, he offered her his arm.

They walked out of the hot, crowded room onto the lawn. Most of the guests had come out of the building and entered the cool of night just as the first fireworks whistled into the sky and burst. The observers made appreciative noises and applauded when a particularly brilliant display went off. Nelleke liked being with Shakespeare. Some phrases from his play rang in her memory. She also wondered what his connection with the Bassano family might be. He performed his dramas and comedies for the nobility, very often for the Queen, who seemed to like his writing. It would only make sense that he would have some acquaintance with the court musicians. His plays, Carmilla had told her, almost always had songs in them and musical interludes. But she thought of his appearance. She wondered if he, like the Bassano family, might be a refugee from Italy. Also an Italian Jew? He had grown up here. Perhaps his father had immigrated. Perhaps, like the Bassano family, he practiced his Jewish religion in secret. She would ask Izaak about it. They watched the fireworks. Wroithsley planned to treat his guests to a banquet when the display was over.

"I'll take my leave," Shakespeare said. "I'm the hired help—not invited to the feast."

He left. A servant appeared and led Nelleke and Dorthea to their designated places at the table.

"We investigated him," Dorthea said.

"Who?"

"Shakespeare. He has a little bit of a record—carried some documents and illegal literature to a couple of men who secreted priests. His father had Roman Catholic sentiments. And a lot of his plays take place in Catholic lands."

"And?"

"He's clear—a loyal Anglican, it appears. I don't think religion is much of concern to him. The investigation was closed."

Nelleke breathed a sigh of relief. A thought occurred to her.

"He looks like he could be Italian. And he's associated with the Bassano family. Could he be an Italian Jew and practice his religion in secret, as they do?"

"He could very well be. We're not concerned with that. The Jews are no threat to us."

Servants brought dishes to the table. The banquet began with eels in a puree flavored with the hot spices merchants were bringing from India and Cathay. The second course featured frumenty pudding and fish. After that, Nelleke and Dorthea ate venison and more fish along with fritters (Nelleke liked these best). They finished with spiced wine and crisp cookies sweetened with honey. Though she could not read Dorthea's mind, she could tell by catching her glance that they were harboring the same thoughts. No one at the table would imagine the two of them needed blood to survive. The various dishes kept their physical frames alive; blood nourished their immortality.

Two men sat across from them: Wriothesley, Earl of South Hampton, and one of his friends name Bennington. Both were forward. Soon they became flirtatious.

"I understand you play for Her Majesty," Wriothesley said.

"I have had that privilege, yes, my Lord."

"You should play for me sometime. I like lute music."

"I'd be delighted." Nelleke knew such an invitation would end up with something more than the lute being played upon.

"We can arrange for an audition, then," Wroithsley said. "Or perhaps a private performance." His eyes flashed slightly when he said this. Nelleke worked hard to suppress the smile that made its way up to her lips. Audition and private performance it would be. Wriothesley had not meant to be ironic.

"I think I would enjoy a private performance—and hopefully I could give you the sort of concert you will always remember." Her smile and the way she leaned forward communicated her intentions.

"Excellent," he beamed. "I'll send word to you, Miss Reitsma."

"Please, call me Nelleke. I'm occupied by day, but at night my time is free."

He smiled. Night, she thought, was the optimal time for what he planned for the two of them to do. "And may I ask what occupies your days?"

"I'm not allowed to say."

Wriothesley had connections in the Queen's court and knew Dorthea worked for Cecil. Nelleke understood he might think she did as well. Things had fallen out auspiciously for her. This would give her a little more space to maneuver.

"Night it will be then, good woman."

They finished the meal and went outside for more fireworks. Wriothesley and Bennington hung near Nelleke and Dorthea. The smoke had just cleared from the first showing of ground pyrotechnics when a servant hurried up and whispered something to Wriothesley. The servant looked harried and spoke quickly and with intensity in his eyes. Wriothesley looked shocked and grave. He gave several rapid commands neither vampire woman could hear to the serving man, who rushed off without taking leave. Soon Nelleke and Dorthea were alone with Bennington. After a moment, a group of house servants pulled up a podium. Wriothesley mounted it and nodded to someone who sounded a trumpet. After several blasts, the crowd grew quiet, curious, and uneasy.

"It is my sad duty to inform all of you," he said, "that Her Majesty, our belovéd Queen, Elizabeth, has died."

A gasp of sorrow, of surprise, anguish, and grief ran through the crowd. Some women wailed and began to weep. Some of the men shed tears as well.

"Propriety requires that our revels end at once," he said. With that, he stepped down. A buzz of confused words ran through the crowd and then the gathering broke up.

XII

Two days after the announcement of Elizabeth's death, Nelleke let Izaak into her bed again. She wanted a lover, and despite his capricious nature and tendency to pursue other women, she decided to take him back in, at least for a while. The two of them had been living together for a month and things had been going fairly well. They had just finished eating after a visit to see Clarice, who had been hosting members of the vampire coven in Yorkshire. Back in her dwelling, Nelleke and Izaak drank and relaxed. She admired his good looks as he lay on the bed bare-chested, his long hair falling over the pillow. Nelleke sat on a chair by the bed. She glanced at her lute, which she kept in her bedchamber. She hoped no one wanted her to play for the Queen's funeral.

"I'm worried about being asked to play for the funeral during the daytime," she said.

"The only place they would have music would be the chapel, which is dark even if the sun is shining—the stained glass will keep out the kind of sunlight that kills us, though it might make you just a little bit weak. I'm sure you can manage to get into the palace before daybreak so that you will already be in place at the appointed time." Izaak stretched. "Will her successor be James of Scotland?"

"That's what Dorthea told me."

He spoke again after a short pause. "I hear Wriothesley

has an eye for you." She bristled at his abruptness.

"And where did you hear that?"

He yawned. "I have my sources."

"As always. Yes, he does seem interested."

"And you?" He looked over at her, meeting her eyes.

"Why do you care?"

He reacted with a look of mild anger. "Well, we are"—

"We are what? A couple? Hardly. You're staying at my house and I'm letting you fuck me now. That doesn't mean we're an item, Izaak. You didn't seem to think about me much all those years you stayed with Denyse. I have plans now."

"You're going to build yourself a staircase of noblemen's beds that ascend to a high place in the royal court like Dorthea has?"

"That pretty much sums it up."

He muttered something in a language she did not know—it was not English, Dutch, or French. He said, in Dutch, "I thought we could mend things."

She answered in English. "You thought you could just stroll back into my life like nothing happened? Don't you think it hurt me when you left?"

"I don't know what I thought."

"Well, maybe you'd better pay more attention to what you think and to what I feel. Some lonely years have passed. I had some affairs, a few lovers, but I never met anyone I felt about like I feel about you."

"What is the problem then?"

"I don't know." She smiled sardonically. "I like London. I like theater, and Wriothesley knows Shakespeare, Jonson, and Kyd. I'm willing to give him what he wants to see some well-done plays."

Izaak frowned. "You seem a little sweet on this Shakespeare fellow too. He doesn't fit exactly into the mode of nobility."

"He's an artist. I love his words."

"He's very close to the Bassano family."

"I'm told. Is he one of your people?"

"I don't think he is. But I wouldn't be surprised if his family was at one time. It's in his blood and he hears it calling." He took a drink of wine, tipping the cup too much so the wine ran in two rivulets down his chin and onto his chest. She got him a damp cloth and threw it to him. He wiped off the spilled wine. "Do you want me to move out?" he asked tossing the cloth back to him.

"You can stay if you want."

"And be one of your many men?"

"I've been one your many women. You leave me for Denyse and then you come back and act like that never happened?"

Izaak got up, dressed, and left in a huff.

Nelleke got her lute out. She often played to sooth herself when she felt weary or upset. As her fingers ran over the fretboard and spilled a cascade of rapid notes into the quiet dark of her bedchamber, she thought about where things were in her life.

She had never stopped loving Izaak, but he needed to know she was not his for the using when he got tired of his latest find. She had let him move in with her—he was not in good financial shape and had spent most of his money trying to impress Denyse. He seemed to think she had taken him in because of his charms and his power over her. Perhaps, she thought as she played, that was true to an extent—but only to an extent. She would not allow him to presume upon her affection.

Nelleke heard a scratching sound. It was coming from the front door. When she put her hand on the latch, she heard meowing and more scratching. She opened the door to see a large tortoise-shell cat that immediately rushed past her feet and scurried to the center of the kitchen. She closed the door and watched it transform into Dorthea.

"You're the only vampire I know who can transform to a cat," Nelleke said.

"It's the only safe way to be out at night. I saw that the Privy Council wants you to play for one of the services for the Queen. Lord Cecil passed the program around to us so we would be on the lookout for infiltrators. I saw you listed as one of the musicians. The event he wants you to play for is during daylight hours."

"I'll find a way to get there. I've been at the palace in the daytime before."

"Yes, but there's something else. You're in danger, Nelleke. You need to go to Devonshire tonight—to Arabella's house."

Nelleke gaped. "Why do I have to go there?"

"I can't tell you. You simply need to go, and you'd better start out now. Your appointment isn't with Arabella, though."

"Dorthea, you're scaring me."

"You need to be scared."

"Who am I going to see? Stop being so mysterious."

"I can't tell you anything more."

"That's a long way to fly and get back."

"You won't be able to come back in one day. Arabella will put you up. You can come back tomorrow night. I'll meet you here. You had better leave right now."

"Dorthea, this is"—

"You trust me, don't you, Nelleke?"

Nelleke paused and let go of her annoyance. "Of course I do. It's just that the look in your eyes makes me think you're sending me into something... bad."

"Not bad, but solemn and maybe a little dangerous. I had hoped you wouldn't get mixed up in all this, but now there is no choice. That's everything I'm allowed to say." Dorthea threw her arms around her friend. "Go on. The person you're going to meet at Arabella's house does not like to be kept waiting. I have to hunt tonight and might not be able to get back to my house in Shoreditch before dawn. May I stay here, at your place?"

"Of course you can. Everything I own is yours, Dorthea."

"You'd better go."

Dorthea kissed her. "You're my best friend. I don't want you to be destroyed. Please go as I've instructed you."

Nelleke held Dorthea a moment and then went out into the night.

Quiet wind greeted her as she transformed to a bat and rose up into the sky. Climbing upward, Nelleke broke through the pale of smoke that hung above the City of London. In the clearer air, she flew more swiftly, gained altitude, and managed to catch the upper winds that carried her along at a good rate of speed. She followed the route of the Thames until it turned north then went straight south until she found the sea. She sent out high-pitched cries and could tell the texture of land or water when they bounced back. Smell and temperature helped her navigate. She skimmed the coast until she came to the estuary of the Exe River and followed it north. She fastened herself to one of the towers at Exeter Cathedral and rested for two hours, took off again, and flew until she recognized the vibrations of woodlands and streams she knew, and then a clearing in the wood. The vibrations indicated shingles on houses and stone chimneys. She smelled smoke. Nelleke swooped to the ground and changed to her human form.

The houses in the clearing sat quiet and dark amid towering trees. Gardens grew, sending the smell of ripening vegetables and herbs to her nose. The din of a thousand crickets, of tree frogs and bullfrogs in the nearby swamp, and a myriad of other nocturnal creatures filled her ears.

She heard something behind her. Before she could turn about, an arm had encircled her. Nelleke tried to resist and then realized she could not move. Whoever had put his arm over her front below her throat and above her breasts had not hurt her and did not seem to be deliberately restraining her. Yet she could not move. She could only hope he meant her no harm.

"You don't have to be afraid," a male voice said. "I won't hurt you."

Nelleke's fear receded. She thought to reply cautiously, but her fiercer side, rising with her annoyance at the skullduggery of this night, ruled her response.

"Well, that's wonderful. You might consider letting me go—if it's not too much trouble."

A small, low laugh sounded and whoever was holding Nelleke released her. She turned. Her eyes fell on the figure of a man—tall—very tall, taller than any man she had seen. He wore a black cloak and stood bareheaded, hair long and brown, face rugged but well-formed, eyes deep-set and piercing.

"I'm getting tired of all this secretive talk," she said. "I want to know who you are. I'm Nelleke Reitsma."

"My name is Devyn."

"I don't know that name. Dorthea knows you and respects you, though she refused to reveal your name me."

"Dorthea is overly dramatic. Let's go inside. Arabella is hunting. She should be back soon."

Nelleke smiled with pleasure at hearing the name of her belovéd friend. The man—Devyn—warmed with her smile.

"Arabella is the most beautiful woman I've known—though I would say, Miss Reitsma, you are as lovely as she, albeit, in a different way."

"Comparing Arabella to me is like comparing the

song of a nightingale to the croak of a bullfrog. You are a charmer, sir. I like that."

"Come. Let's go inside."

The rustic interior of the home, with its touch of sophisticated décor and styling, reminded Nelleke of Arabella, who had been a lady, mistress to Henry VIII, but then had returned to become a wild woman of the wood—a huntress like Artemis (though far from chaste). She assumed Devyn and Arabella were lovers.

"You've had a long flight. I'm sure you'll welcome refreshment. Wine?"

"That would be wonderful."

He took off his cloak and crossed the room to a rack of wine bottles. In the dim light of three oil lamps, Devyn looked even taller and more formidable than he had looked outside. He poured a pewter cup of red wine for Nelleke and one for himself. He lifted the mug.

"A toast—to understanding."

She nodded, touched her vessel to his, and drank. Nelleke had drunk innumerable toasts and had thought of them as polite functions of parties and dinner. The look in Devyn's eyes as he nodded in response to touching the mugs suggested he attributed something sacred to the action—something joyous and celebratory, but also solemn. She wondered how old he was. She had noticed the same look in the eyes of Clarice and Bertrand, both of whom had lived in medieval times and earlier.

"Yes," he said, startling her. "I'm older than either of the two people you just thought of—older than Clarice, older than Bertrand."

A chill of fear and surge of resentment ran through Nelleke, though she tried to appear unruffled. Then she realized the foolishness of putting on such an appearance. If he could read her thoughts, any deceptions would be pointless.

"I didn't know you were reading my mind."

"It's not that exactly. I'm not peering into your thoughts like a voyeur staring in a window. When something needs to be clarified, though, or resolved, I know it."

"Will you tell me why you've brought me here?"

"I brought you here for more than one reason. I brought you because you need protection. The Privy Council wants you to play for the Queen's memorial service. Afterward, they plan to retain you for 'questioning.' You don't want to be questioned by them."

"How did this happen, my Lord?"

"Dispense with 'my Lord.' We're equals, even if we recognize that some of us have higher responsibilities and perhaps more wisdom from long years on earth. I am head of the Coven of England."

Nelleke gasped. Despite Devyn's admonition, she wanted to kneel before him. He smiled.

"We're equals—brothers and sisters. Do you think you would like to work for the English government, Nelleke?"

Not fully recovered from the double shock of finding out her life was in danger and finding herself speaking with the head vampire of the Isle of Britannia. She could only stare.

"Cat got your tongue?"

She snapped out of her amazement.

"No, I"—she looked up. She had to snap out of this lethargy. "I'm sorry. But this is too much at once—and I'm tired from the long flight here. I want to know how the government discovered me."

"Do you know Dorthea is an agent for the Crown?"

"Yes. But she maintains secrecy about being among the undying—doesn't she?"

"She does, but Lord Cecil and most of the higher-ranking Lords of the Council know her true nature. Cecil and a few others deal with me. They know who—and what—I am. The Queen was quite taken with your music. You're friends with Dorthea. You only perform at night and when you're required to be there by day, you get a room. The lie you told about how your eyes and flesh react to sunlight didn't fool anyone. They're very careful about who they let into the presence of the Queen. The fact that you kept your identity secret made them see you as a danger. They very much want to follow the Queen's last wishes because they respected her so. But afterward, they planned to expose you to light so you would die. But they came to me first."

Nelleke felt lightheaded. Devyn helped her to a chair.

"They came to me first with a proposition. If you agree to become an operative of the government—to do what Dorthea and I and a few others do for them—they won't go after you. Are you open to this proposition, Nelleke?"

"Do I have any choice?"

"You could flee, I suppose, but that would be difficult. They're watching you. They have lots of eyes and informers and spies everywhere. You would have to leave England. That in itself could be difficult, though I think if you really wanted to get away you probably could. But to leave everything you have here would break your spirit. If you work for them, you could stay in London—and thrive."

"Who was behind Carmilla's arrest and torture?" she asked abruptly. Mention of London and the fact that Devyn had access to information most people would never know made Nelleke bold to ask. The question had been on her mind since Carmilla's exile. Devyn looked serious and, Nelleke fancied, a little fearful.

"I don't know. I'm trying to find out. Lord Cecil can't discover anything about whoever it was. The Queen didn't know of it—or if she did, she chose not to reveal what she knew. The threat of Aldebaran is ended, thanks in good part to your bravery. But someone had the jewel. Even though we have neutralized it as a threat, the people who used it against Carmilla are still at large. If they were able to access the Tower of London, they have political ties. If Cecil doesn't know who they were, they have considerable influence or know powerful magic; maybe both. Hopefully, we will find out who they are and destroy them."

Just then the door opened and Arabella came in.

Nelleke and Arabella shared a long embrace. As always, Nelleke felt her friend's strength suffuse her own spirit. She reveled in Arabella's beauty: her tall, strong body, well-toned arms, broad shoulders, and slender but powerful torso; her sturdy, sculpted legs covered with hair; the determined but, paradoxically, gentle and wistful expression on her pretty face; the long, brown locks that fell past her shoulders.

They kissed. Arabella went over to Devyn and kissed him—a lover's kiss, not the sister's kiss she had shared with Nelleke. She looked small next to his large, strong body. Nelleke wondered what sort of lover he might be.

As the three of them drank more wine and talked, Arabella said she had hunted down a murderer the authorities had been trying to apprehend for the last two years.

"You're hunting human victims now?" Nelleke asked. Like many wodies—woodland vampires—Arabella had preyed on animals.

"It's easier," Arabella said, "and I don't have to hunt every two weeks. Human blood makes me feel stronger. I do like Izaak and only destroy those who are destructive themselves. The people in Exeter will be safer because I fed on a certain victim tonight. And I'm good for the next two months."

Most vampires who preyed on humans had to eat once a month, not once every two months. But Arabella was in such magnificent shape and so strong her body probably more efficiently processed the blood she drank.

They had more wine. It made Nelleke sleepy. Weariness from flying so far overwhelmed her. As she nodded in her

chair, a girl—she could not have been older than fourteen—
came in.

"This is Githa," Arabella said. "She only recently
crossed over. I'm teaching her. She went on her first solo
hunt tonight. Githa, this is my friend, Nelleke." She turned.
"Nelleke, you don't mind sharing a bed with Githa, do you?"

Nelleke said she didn't. Even though Githa was still a
little wild and invigorated from hunting, she was ready to
turn in. The two of them washed and settled in the guest bed.
Weary as she was, Nelleke asked Githa where she was from.

"Northumberland. Some people up there found out
about me after I crossed over. They were going to drive a
stake through my heart. I fled and met Arabella." Nelleke
could see the girl smile in the dark. "She was walking on a
woodland road in the middle of the night. I actually attacked
her. I found out pretty quickly she was not mortal and not
a woman to be trifled with. She helped me find food that
night. I was almost insane with hunger. She took me in and
became my angel."

"I imagine she would be a good teacher."

"She saved me from destruction. I feel confident I can
set out on my own now."

"Where will you go?"

"Up north again. I met a young man from Cumbria. I
might go up and live with him." She paused and asked in a
more serious tone. "Are you the woman who managed to
seize the Emerald of Argruna's wrath?"

The phrase intrigued Nelleke.

"If you mean Aldebaran, yes. I helped secure it. I was
the one who carried it out of the Tower of London. Several
people assisted me."

"You resisted its spell?"

"I guess I did. I don't know how."

"You are powerful in spirit."

"That may be. If I am, I don't know how I got that

way. You called the jewel the Emerald of Argruna's Wrath. The others called it Aldebaran."

"Isn't Aldebaran a star that shines in the summer sky?"

"It is," Nelleke answered. "That's what the Coven of London called the jewel."

"Maybe it is also called that," Githa murmured.

Sleep claimed Nelleke. When she woke in the night, Githa was washing. She had a slender, beautiful body, long blonde hair, and fair skin. Nelleke heard noise and realized Arabella and Devyn were enjoying some morning delight. Githa giggled.

"They swyve at this time every night," she said, using the older, regional term for the deed. "He's a marvelous man. I've had him several times. He'll probably want to tumble you before you leave. If he does, Arabella won't mind. He laid me once and I could hear her in the kitchen humming a song and cooking while we sported. When we were finished, all three of us sat down and enjoyed a pleasant meal together."

Nelleke washed as Githa dressed. Night had settled on the forest clearing. She heard Arabella get her joy; Devyn shortly followed. Nelleke and Githa walked outside to fetch water from a nearby spring. Stars blazed. She caught sight of the constellation Taurus where Aldebaran shone so brightly.

"Where did you say your family was from, Githa?"

"Northumberland. I come from an old family that owns land. We even have a castle. We don't live in it, thank God, but it stands on a hill not far from our house. We go back a long way. That's how I got my old-fashioned name. *Githa* means *war* in the ancient tongue. So my name means 'warrior maiden.'"

"It's a beautiful name," Nelleke said as they filled buckets with icy spring water. When they returned, Devyn and Arabella were up and around. Arabella squatted by the hearth and stirred a pot. Nelleke smelled porridge. Bacon sizzled on a spit. The smell of food, the presence of her own kind, the warmth and coziness of Arabella's home, made her feel secure.

They ate. Nelleke enjoyed being with Arabella. She remembered when they met, just before the ceremony inducting Dorthea into the world of the undead. After Nelleke followed her, Arabella had acted as her angel, teaching her the intricacies of living as a vampire. Izaak had helped her along the path as well, but Arabella had been her primary mentor. Thinking of Izaak raised Nelleke's resentment. She stifled it, not wanting to look angry during the meal.

When breakfast ended Devyn went off to write letters introducing Githa to the Coven of the North. Their realm encompassed a territory consisting of five shires—Northumberland, Yorkshire, Westmorland, Cumberland, and Lancashire. A vast territory, very few of the undead lived there despite the fact that it was remote, rural, and afforded innumerable places for concealment and hunting. The vampires there had been hunted and killed for centuries, so much that only a handful had survived. The City of Exeter, Arabella told Nelleke, had more vampires in and around it than the huge area the Coven of the North governed.

"Why were so many of us hunted down up there?"

"No one knows. It is a little unsettling, though."

They cleared the table, scraped the dishes, and fed the scraps to the small herd of pigs Arabella kept. By the time they returned to her house, the caldron of water they had hung over the fireplace had heated. They began washing dishes.

"How much do you know about Githa?" Nelleke asked.

"Not much more than she probably told you. I like her. She seems like a sweet girl."

"She is. I like her too. But she called the gem that had such terrible power the Emerald of Argruna's wrath. Everyone else called it Aldebaran. She knew Aldebaran was the name of a star, but used the other term for the jewel. She knew it was an emerald. She said she had only heard it called by the name she used for it. Who is Argruna?"

"A goddess they worshipped up that way—a Welsh goddess. I know that because my former husband, Jakyn, was Welsh. He told me about her once. Of course, no one worships her now that the old religions are gone."

Nelleke still felt puzzlement. "Why would she call the stone by that name? Everyone in our coven called it Aldebaran—even Clarice called that, and she's the oldest vampire in London. She goes all the way back to Edward the Confessor and crossed over before the Normans conquered the land."

"Maybe she knew what it was called in the old days but just used the name for it everyone else was using. But Githa is one of us." Arabella smiled. "She tried to attack me."

"Yes she told me about that," Nelleke laughed. "At least she attacked the right person. She's a very beautiful young lady. She said her family went back to ancient days. Do you know much about them?"

"They're the house of Percy."

"I'm Dutch, Arabella, and I don't know anything about the noble houses of England."

"They're an ancient family that has governed the north of England since the Conquest. They're powerful and wealthy. The Kings of England have always feared them."

Nelleke fell silent wondering about the jewel that had exuded so much hatred and anger so much evil energy, but also, a note of love and tenderness.

XIII

While Arabella cooked and tidied her house, Nelleke and Devyn sat on a fallen tree near a small, rocky stream and talked. One of the marvelous things about being a vampire, Nelleke smiled to herself, was that creatures of the night knew you were alive but also seemed to have some knowledge of the ferocity and invulnerability that lay just beyond the energies they could smell and sense. So they stayed away from you. Mosquitos, biting flies, and, more seriously, snakes and large predators, let you alone. The two of them sat on a log swarming with carpenter ants that did not crawl on or bite them. The moon rode full in a welkin festooned with stars. In London, it was hard to see the stars due to smoke and fog. Here they shone in all their magnificence. Devyn had brought out a wineskin and two goblets. Nelleke took a drink of the full, red vintage.

"May I ask you, Devyn, how old you are?"

"I hope not too old for you. I have walked the soil of England for more than two-thousand years. I fought the Romans when they first arrived. To me, the Norman Conquest is modern history! When I went on guard duty one night on the edge of a swamp, a woman—a *Roman* woman, God save us—brought me into the kingdom with her embrace."

Nelleke laughed. "Embrace? That's an odd way to put it."

"Well, she pretended to be a whore. Pleasure first, and then she attacked me. But, the second part was an embrace as well—to satisfy hunger; and yet, when she perceived I had become one of her own kind, she immediately carried me to safety. Her name was Livia."

"Is she still with us?"

"She went back to Rome. She lives in Perugia now. I see her when I go there."

"Do you travel much?"

"Not often. It's too much bother to arrange things, so I tend to stay home. Many tasks need tending to in Albion."

She noted that, like Clarice, he used the Roman name for Britain.

"What would those tasks be?"

"The Privy Council—which is the real seat of power in England—tolerates us because we are useful to them. Otherwise, they see us as cursed souls and spawn of the Devil. Never forget that. Always give yourself a means of escape your employers will not know about. If you agree to the proposition I've brought you, you will deal mostly with me. Still, it's wise to be cautious."

"I don't feel like I have much choice but to accept."

"If you throw your lot in with us, you'll have protected status. And the Privy Council pays well. You would not have to worry about money."

In her early days among the undead, Nelleke realized that being a vampire did not release one from the tasks of living. You had to have a place to stay, food to eat in the times you were in a phase that you did not need blood, clothes and accessories. She robbed her victims, but never knew how much gold they would have on them. So far she had been lucky and lived comfortably off what she took from her prey. It would be marvelous to have a more predictable source of income.

"What sorts of things would I do for them?"

"If you work for the Privy Council, you will be called upon to assassinate enemies of the state. That's what they hire us to do. I know something of your morality. Arabella said you and Izaak only prey upon those you consider evil-doers, so it might be a conflict for you, and I would only want you to agree to this if you knew you could do what is expected of you."

"What sorts of enemies would they want me to eliminate?"

"Today it often has to do with religion. England has broken ties with the Church of Rome and founded its own church. The Roman Church smuggles priests and teachers into the land to convert the people back to the old ways. They also bring in literature that is outlawed by the English Church. Wealthy English who secretly adhere to the old faith assist and harbor infiltrators from the Continent. Your job might be to expose these people—as your friend Dorthea does—in which case they will be executed or imprisoned and their monies and estates confiscated; or you may be called upon to kill someone the state considers an enemy but does not want to taint its hands with eliminating them."

"I suppose," Nelleke said, "they would constitute some sort of threat if the Privy Council considers them enemies."

"To the state, yes; to us, no."

"I'm not sure, Devyn."

"The Council knows you're one of the undying. You wormed your way into the palace and into the Queen's very chamber, which is more than a little disturbing to them. If you were working for them—if I could certify that you would cooperate with the way they use all of us—that would make you safe. As it stands now, they don't know what to think of you—but they know you're a vampire, they know you can get into the palace, and I can't assure them that you are working for their purposes. They are quite capable of hunting you down. It would difficult for you to hide from them."

"So my choice is to do what they say, whether I think it's right or not, or to let them destroy me."

"More or less—or to run, which would be dangerous."

"And you can stop them from doing that?"

"If I tell them you will do their bidding, and if you do, you won't have to worry about the anything. Work as an agent for them like Dorothea, I, and a few others do, and you'll be safe."

After a long silence, she said, "I'll have to think about it."

"You need to let me know today. They plan to expose you to light after you play at the Queen's funeral, and if you don't show up they will know you're on to them and intensify the search for you. They might not be able to find you, Nelleke, but living a life on the run, or in exile, is not pleasant."

She nodded. "Give me some time to think about it. I'll let you know soon."

He nodded. They sat in silence for a time. Neither of them wanted to go inside. The beauty of the starry sky held them in its spell. After a while, Nelleke decided to ask Devyn about something that had been bothering her.

"You lived in ancient times, Devyn—in pagan times. Did you know of the goddess Argruna?"

"Of course. People in the east and north worshipped her, especially in Wales, Northumberland, and South Scotland. Why?"

Nelleke told him about how Githa had called Aldebaran "the Emerald of Argruna's Wrath."

"Odd," he said after listening carefully to her story. "I've never heard that term used for the Stone of Aldebaran, but there is legend that the goddess Argruna loved a girl who was pledged as a priestess of her order. A vampire killed the girl, leaving the goddess grief-stricken and angry. The story goes no further."

"What was she the goddess of?"

"Of War and Slaughter. Warriors called on her before they went into battle. Common people evoked her name when they slaughtered an animal."

"When I was in the Tower and subject to the spell of the stone, I sensed anger, malevolence, but also a small, dulcet strain—like music—like a song of love or tender lament."

"That would be in keeping with the goddess's nature. She had a gentle side, but she was also a violent goddess exalting in blood and death."

"You speak of her in past tense. Has she completely faded?"

"Many of the old gods are gone now. Not all of them. But Argruna faded long before the Church came to the Isle of Albion. No one knows why."

"I wonder if she created the stone to avenge herself upon our race. I wonder if she put so much of her soul and power into it that she ceased to exist except that she exists through the stone so that vengeance is the only expression of her godhood."

"That would be plausible—though it is not a concern now that the stone is ours. Maybe we should ask Githa about it."

"Well be sure to do that." Devyn paused and then added, "I hope you will be willing to work with us," Devyn said. "Arabella speaks highly of you."

"Arabella is one of the kindest, most beautiful women I know."

"Quite beautiful," Devyn agreed. "She is strong as a warrior maiden, swift as a deer, wild as the wood in which she dwells—and ravishing—more so for me because she follows the ancient ways. I hadn't stroked the hair on a beautiful woman's legs for a thousand years until I met up with her."

They laughed, finished their wine, and went inside. They

questioned Githa, but she knew nothing more than that the emerald was named after the Goddess Argruna, and that in pagan times her family had worshipped that particularly deity. After the noonday meal, she departed for the northern English climes.

XIV

Nelleke returned to London. She had agreed to work for the Privy Council. After her decision, things fell into place with what she considered remarkable speed. The Privy Council arranged for her to have a room in the palace—an interior room in the lower depths with no outside windows. They also gave her a purse of gold. She met Lord Cecil, the director of Elizabeth's (soon to be James') secret service. He was cordial but, Nelleke thought, eyed her as if at any moment she might sprout horns and a tail and leap at him to drag him down to perdition.

Devyn said the stained glass in the chapel would filter out any destructive rays of the sun. If the sun shone bright, she might feel a little short of breath but could manage it.

The day turned out to be gloomy. Nelleke walked from her room down darkened corridors and secret tunnels to the chapel. A huge crowd of men in suits, hats and long capes, all black (Devyn among them), and women in somber gowns of burgundy and purple, veils over their faces, jammed the chapel. Servants wore black bands on their arms. A choir in black robes sang psalms and lamentations. Clergy read scripture. The usual bright clothing, the baubles and gold, plumes and braid, were not to be seen, though Devyn had told her the rich had special rings and bracelets with dark jewels (bloodstone, onyx, ruby) made for the occasion. Those close to the Queen delivered eulogies. At last the time came for Nelleke to play. She wore a black gown and crepe over her face. She even hung a black ribbon from the tuning head of her lute. A servant placed a chair for her. She sat, took up her lute, and played a lament John Bull had written for the occasion.

The notes filled the room, suffusing it with wistful sadness. The tune traveled through the lofty interior's silence. Nelleke felt the audience respond with restrained emotion. She played carefully, expressively, letting the evocative power of the lament work its melancholy spell. When Nelleke finished, an almost inaudible sigh rang through the room. Nelleke bowed and returned to her room. A bag of gold and another bag containing three expensive rings lay on her bed. She felt she had made a good impression.

She settled back, waited for nightfall, and departed for her home. When she entered, she heard swishing and shuffling. She saw a cat and then remembered Dorthea. Her friend transformed to her human shape and smiled. Nelleke returned the smile.

"*Welkom ann boord*," Dorthea said.

"*Dus ik op enn schip nu ben?*"

Dorthea laughed. "Yes, you're on a ship, my friend," she answered, still speaking *Nederlands*. "You will sail some rough seas, but the pay is good and the amenities luxurious."

"I've been paid twice as much in a week as I've taken off my victims in all the time I've lived in England. So I will agree that the amenities are good."

"Devyn, with Lord Cecil's approval, made me your contact. I have your first assignment."

"Sit down. I'll get some wine."

They drank and gossiped. Carmilla, Dorthea had learned through her network of informers, living and undead, had gone to live in Steinemark, in South Austria, in the vicinity of Graz. The remote mountains and thick forests of that part of the world would be good for her,

Dorthea said. Nelleke talked about playing at the Queen's memorial service. Dorthea had met King James.

"What's he like?"

She rolled her eyes. "I'm not impressed. He's small and thin, beady-eyed, and looks scruffy no matter how much he dresses up. I'm also disturbed that he has a rather militant view on our side of things."

"What do you mean by that?"

"He published a book called *Daemonology*. He conducted some witchcraft trials when he was King of Scotland. He thinks some massive conspiracy of dark forces is hiding out in his new realm."

"Well, he's right about that. Should we leave?"

Dorthea gave a sly smile. "No need. We have a King and Parliament, but then there are those who truly rule the country. Whatever happens to the poor, wretched souls he convicts of witchcraft and tortures to death, the Privy Council will protect us. They depend on us too much to let any ill befall us."

"I hope you're right."

"Don't worry about it. If he goes after witches, you and I will probably be the ones commissioned to hunt them down."

Nelleke did not think of killing innocent people in such a cavalier manner. Dorthea had not always been this way, and Nelleke wondered what might have changed her perspective so much. She resolved that no matter how deceptive or bloody she had to be to survive her work with the Privy Council, she would not allow herself to become callous and cruel. She would disappear—go back to the Netherlands or to France - before she became indifferent to what little morality was left for her to embrace.

"What is my assignment?" she asked, hoping Dorthea did not tell her it was an assassination.

"You're being sent to Northumberland. The Crown's

agents suspect that a large section of the Percy family is practicing the Roman religion, but investigators can't find any hard evidence for the charge. That will be your task."

"What am I supposed to do?"

"You're to infiltrate their house and look for evidence of violation—secret rooms where Catholic clergy are concealed, hidden chapels, books that teach forbidden doctrine or incite disobedience to the King. You have a contact at the house of William Percy, who is the prime suspect in the matter. She's a servant girl. She isn't one of us, but she will help you."

"I'll do what I can."

"You can begin your journey tonight. Be cautious. The family is wary and suspicious. You need to be extremely secretive."

A few hours later, Nelleke began her journey. She flew as a bat by night. Dorthea provided her with a list of places to stop and rest: safe houses and caves. The journey took a week. Finally, in the small hours of morning, the moon full in a cool, starry sky, Nelleke came down above the grass sward in front of a large, ancient house, materialized into her human form, and stood gazing at the location of her assignment. Weary from travel, she perhaps stood too long. She heard dogs snarling and turned to see two mastiffs bellowing and bearing down on her.

She transformed to a mist—remembering all Arabella had taught her. The house, a moment earlier bathed in moonlight, suddenly dimmed, surrounded by a dark swirl of vapor. The dogs halted, confused, their baying having died down to whimpers.

Existing as a mist still bewildered Nelleke. When she changed to a bat, she was still a living creature; you could compare and equate human functions to those you experienced in the animal. When she turned to a non-human substance, no such comparable categories existed;

perception operated through modes she could not express and hardly understood. Somehow, though, she moved to her destination, going in an upward trajectory toward a set of geometric constructs, her shapeless form contrasting to fixed places, porous to solid. Lost to gravity, weight, and substance, not thinking but somehow perceiving and moving toward an understood goal, she continued on. Anyone outside would have merely seen the mist rise and dissolve. Nelleke felt herself swirl, tumble (up, not down), congeal, and then lurch back into her human form. Thought and perception returned.

The geometric constructs had been the rectangles of open windows and the square shape of a room. In the times of vampire dominance, she could see in the dark, but, as Arabella had told her, this sort of "seeing" was different—things existed as concepts rather than shapes. Her gaze fell on the idealized form of a woman lying in bed. Now she saw the sight of what she had sensed conceptually: a woman lying in bed. She looked maybe eighteen years old, chubby, with red hair and ruddy skin. Nelleke came to her bedside, knelt silently, and whispered the name Dorthea had given her.

"Kaylein. Kaylein."

The girl stirred and started awake. Nelleke put one hand over her mouth and one on her shoulder.

"Quiet. Don't cry out. The Privy Council dispatched me here. Dorthea sent me. You are my contact here. Do you know what I'm talking about?"

Eyes large with fear, the girl nodded. Nelleke removed her hand. The girl stared at Nelleke's naked body.

"I'm sorry I frightened you."

"How did you get into my chamber, mistress? The house is guarded and the door bolted."

"I transformed into a mist. I'm naked because when I do that, my clothing doesn't transform with me. I hope you have something I can wear. I'll conceal myself during the day. At night I'll come out and search for what I've been sent to investigate."

Kaylein found her a very nicely cut dress another serving woman had left behind. In a wealthy house, the higher-ranking servants dressed richly, and as she put on the garment Kaylein found for her, Nelleke delighted at its beauty and in the fact that it fit so well. She also gave her shoes and hose. Only the knickers she got, which were from Kaylein's wardrobe, were a little too big. She wondered who would find the simple frock she had left lying in a heap on the front lawn when she transformed to a mist.

"Good," she said. "Thank you, Kaylein. Have you seen anything?"

"A few things, mistress, though the family is guarded about it. I am not a high-ranking servant. The only thing I notice is messengers bringing in books—not large quantities of them, but they have brought in quite a few. They handle them carefully, as if they are quite valuable. The people in this house are not scholars and do not value learning. The Master here can hardly read. The Mistress, I think, cannot read at all. Yet thick volumes are brought in and handled with utmost care. And they are brought in with some secrecy."

"Someone is reading them—a scholar they're harboring?"

"Perhaps. I've seen nothing more."

"You've been helpful." Nelleke pondered a moment. "Where are the books deposited? Do you know? Is there a library?"

"There is a library from ancient days. In all my years here I've never seen the Master or the Mistress go into it."

"Then it would be a good place to hide someone."

"Yes, my lady." Kaylein answered, "The door is bolted shut. I've tried to get into it myself, but I can't budge the lock."

"I have ways of getting where I need to be. I will go now. You'll see me from time to time. Go back to sleep. I want to explore the house and gain an idea of the lay of the building. Where is the library?"

"Second floor. Take the rear stairwell outside the door to this room, descend two flights, and you will come to the main corridor. The library is the middle door with the carved images at the entryway. They are images of ancient deities. Be cautious, lady. Evil things dwell in this house."

"No one is more aware of that than I."

Nelleke found her way to the corridor. Paintings and wooden carving of ancient Percies lined it. The statues flanking the library door depicted Artemis and Apollo, though the female sculpture did not look as much like a classic Greek carving as the male figure did. She tried the door. True to Kaylein's word, it was strongly secured. Transforming to mist inside would be dangerous and she would once again need to find clothes to wear; it was an exhausting, troublesome transformation and she needed her wits and her strength. Nelleke decided to break the lock. She drew on her vampire strength. As she did so, she felt her fangs and talons form. She grasped the door handle and turned it until she heard it snap. The loud metallic crack sounded through the silence of night. Nelleke waited, wondering if anyone had heard. When no one appeared to investigate, she went inside.

She knew at once the room was being used. Its bookshelves were clean. The surface of the large table in the center of it had been dusted. A tall window closed off with curtains rose opposite the table; its curtains were clean and looked new. Nelleke walked about looking for doors and perhaps a false wall that would conceal a "priest's hole." She found nothing, but her eyes were drawn to a stack of books covered with black cloth. She removed the cloth and peered into the top volume.

The pages looked blank until she turned and a curtain fluttered enough to send a beam of moonlight to the page. She saw letters in the light that fell on the book. When the curtain closed once more, the page showed blank.

Puzzled, Nelleke went to the window and pulled back the curtain. Moonlight suffused the room and writing covered the pages of the book. Somehow, the letters only appeared when the moon shone on the book's leaves. Nelleke held her hand over the page. The letters disappeared in the shape of her hand and formed once more when she took it away and the moonlight shone on them once more. The letters were odd: elongated, angular, ornate. They were written in silver ink in a language unknown to her.

The night had waned. She needed to get out of the house and to the safe location to which Dorthea had directed her. She took the volume with the strange letters, covered the pile of books with the black cloth, and hurried out of the library and out of the house.

The book tucked under her arm, she made her way across the sward toward the woodland river a half mile from the house.

She heard snarling. The dogs. She had forgotten about them. Nelleke could not transform or she would have to abandon the book. The huge, black mastiffs closed on her. Her vampire strength and speed asserted itself. She whirled about, surprising the dogs with her speed. She kicked one, hearing its ribs snap as it whined loudly. The second she struck with her hand, knocking it unconscious. The third leaped at her. Nelleke caught it with her free hand, closed her elbow about its neck, and suffocated it until it was unconscious. She dropped the still form of the creature, turned to pick up the garment, shoes, and undergarments she had left behind when she turned into a mist, and hurried to the wood that lay past the smooth lawn in front of the house.

She hoped no one had heard the melee. Inside the line of trees, she slowed, pulled up her skirts, and, using a set of dry stepping stones, cross a small, shallow stream.

Following the creek to an odd stone formation—a circle of upright monoliths casting long shadows in the moonlight—Nelleke turned and found a stone path Devyn had instructed her to look for. She followed this, noting the sky had begun to lighten. Feeling short of breath from the tiny trace of sunlight, she hurried along. Relief filled her heart when she saw an ancient house built into the side of a hill, also just as Devyn had described it. She ran for the door. Once inside, she relaxed and breathed out a thankful sigh.

"You made it."

Nelleke screamed and turned. Devyn stood in the dark recesses of the house. Nelleke relaxed.

"Good God! You frightened me so much I pissed my pants!"

He laughed. "I'm sorry." He went to her and put his arms around her. She rested against him and began to cry. Devyn held her, patting her as she wept. "Rough time of it?" he asked when she had calmed down.

"The watchdogs attacked me. I had to sneak around the house. I transformed to a mist, which always exhausts me. I had to hurt the dogs. That will raise suspicion."

"The task you accepted is fraught with dangers. What's the book you're holding?"

She told him about it. He set it on a table in the middle of the sun-proof room.

"Let me fetch some water from the river. We can wash. We'll wash your knickers too."

"It's getting light outside."

"I'll have time to gather water. You can undress while I get it."

He left with a wooden bucket. Nelleke pulled off her dress and undergarments. She left on the shoes. She had soaked the underwear Kaylein had given her. Hearing Devyn's voice in what she had assumed would be an empty room had terrified her, making Nelleke realize how tense and frightened she was. She hung her knickers and dress on a hook she found, standing naked (but for her shoes) in the quiet, secure room. She knew what would happen when he returned. No reason to imagine it would be otherwise. Arabella would not know—and even if she found out, she would not think it a betrayal. Vampire reactions were different from those of living humans. Devyn's position as Head Vampire of England demanded she yield to him. And she wanted to.

He returned with a bucket of water and gently washed her with a cloth. She shivered, cried out, and laughed when the cold water touched her flesh. He dried her off, washed her knickers, and hung them up. After they had made love, Devyn dressed and Nelleke wrapped up in a blanket. The two of them looked at the book. Its pages were blank.

"I've never seen them before," Devyn said, "and I'm not seeing them now, but I know they are moon runes. They were written in ink that only reflects moon and starlight. Such letters were written in the ancient days, long before Christianity came to Albion and Hibernia. You say you found this book in the library at the Percy house?"

"A stack of books sat on the table there. The others looked like books on sorcery and magic. I hope they don't miss the book I brought here. I had to break the lock to get into the room. That will make them wary as well."

"I doubt if they miss the book. The Percies aren't big readers. But whoever is reading it might tell them it's missing. If they are hiding a fugitive and he has to come out of hiding to tell them one of his books is missing, that might give us the opportunity we need to find whoever it is they're concealing."

By this time, Nelleke was too exhausted to listen or

talk. They bedded down and woke when night had fallen. They made love once more. Nelleke felt joy, pleasure, but, oddly, satisfaction that she had fulfilled her obligation. As the senior vampire in England, Devyn symbolized the continuity of their tribe—a tribe outside the foundations of morality and the restraints humans placed upon themselves. When they lay together they rehearsed not only passion but duty. Nelleke felt as much fulfillment and satisfaction from the one as from the other.

When she slipped into the Percy house the next night, sneaking in an open door, she heard servants talking about what happened to the dogs. She had trouble understanding their northern accents but caught most of it.

"Must have been a bear," one said.

"Ain't no bear around here."

"What else could have done it?"

"I don't know. But not a bear. Ain't been bear in these woods since Edward was King."

"At least it didn't kill them."

"It hurt old Snarler pretty bad."

Nelleke lurked in the shadows, listening for anything they said that might be helpful to her mission.

"When do those fops from London get here?" a female voice asked.

"They're here," the reply came. "Odd-looking bunch. Wouldn't trust any of them."

"Never trust actors." Her ears perked up when she heard this. She slipped past the knot of gossiping servants. Going through the candle-lit corridors of the house, she peaked around a corner and saw Shakespeare. He supervised a group of players, advising them on how to act out their roles. *This is not good*, she thought. *If he sees me I'll have to make up a story about why I'm here.* Then her mouth fell open and her heart fluttered. Giles, her son-in-law, was there; and, watching him from the sidelines, arms crossed, a smile of smug, satisfied pride on her face, Anita.

Shit, Nelleke whispered to herself. *Shit, shit, shit, shit, shit.*

Moving cautiously, she followed the maze of halls, corridors, and passageways until she came to what looked like a main corridor. Before she had taken two steps into it, a guard with a hauberk caught her by the arm.

"Hold, woman. Who are you and what are you doing here?"

Nelleke caught her breath and gathered her wits.

"I'm one of the players," she lied. "I was told the room in which we are to perform is in this part of the house."

He looked her over. "A woman player? Well, I suppose you're telling the truth. That Shakespeare is letting women on the stage is the buzz since your troupe arrived. The play will be performed in the Tapestry Room, just past the library where the statues are." He pointed.

"Thank you, Master. Shakespeare wanted me to inspect it."

He cocked his head toward two marble statues down the hallway. Nelleke hurried away from him. Passing the library, she heard voices. It sounded like an argument. She slipped into what the guard had called the Tapestry Room, closed and bolted the door and looked about. She found what she had hoped to find: a vent window that connected the two rooms. She put her ear near it, careful to conceal herself (it was only a square designed to permit the circulation of air through the rooms). Her abilities kicked in, heightening her hearing. She listened: two female voices and one male voice spoke.

"I can't believe you permitted him to destroy that book!" a female voice said.

"He claims he didn't destroy it. He did go through our library and removed what he deemed the literature of heathens or books that taught black magic but says he destroyed none of them."

"Then where is the book of runes?"

"Stolen. Someone broke into the library last night. Snapped the lock."

"You know that only one kind of creature would have the strength to do that. It probably hurt the dogs as well. If we don't find that book, we're done for, William. That meddling priest you're hiding under the table has done us all in. If we don't have the book, we can't find out where the goddess is and can't contact her. She's dormant, like the moon when it is new and shining no light. To empower her and free her from her dormant form we have to read the spell written in the runes. After years of searching, someone finally found it for us, and almost immediately it risks being lost. We must have the book to free the goddess. There is no other way."

Silence followed.

"You're afraid of him, aren't you?" the female voice continued. "He's frightened you with stories of hellfire and damnation. I'll warn you that the wrath of Argruna will be more to bear than any tale your clergy may tell you. Can you imagine how angry she will be if you end her worship? For six-hundred years our family has maintained the shrine. One-hundred and fifty-one priestesses who consecrated themselves to the goddess are buried in the woods about this house. I stand in that order of priestesses and serve as they served. And as your kinswoman and a priestess of this order, I declare to you that if you abandon the shrine, their ghosts will arise and torment you. A curse will bring ruin upon this house. Fear it. Fear it, I say."

"We don't know where the book is. Father Hooper didn't destroy it. How could he have even known what it said? Or seen the letters?"

"If he saw them disappear when the moon went down, he would naturally see it as sorcery."

"He is a man of truth. Someone else has the book."

"If the undead have it, our reign here is ended. They have the emerald of Argruna's Wrath—meaning they have the goddess prisoner. Only we can free her and unleash her wrath against their kind, as we did in the days of King Henry II. But we must have the book. Reciting the spell from memory is not efficacious. It must be read from the silver runes or the magic will not work. It had to have been one of the accursed drinkers of human blood who broke into this house, stole the book, almost killed the dogs, and are even now lurking in the corridors. You need to search for them."

"With the acting troupe here, that will be difficult."

A long pause came. The female voice said, "This is the end of the world."

Nelleke heard more whispered discourse. She knew she had to do two things: contact Devyn, and find out who the priestess was and where she lived. The meeting in the other room had broken up. She thought a moment and stepped out into the hall as the party from the library emerged.

Nelleke glanced at them before she knelt. She had seen etchings of the Lord and Lady of the House and recognized them. A tall woman—very tall—in a plain white dress stood beside them. Her eyes fixed on Nelleke.

"Who are you, woman, are what are you doing here?"

"Please you, my Lord and Ladies. I work for Master Shakespeare's troupe."

"You are one of the female actors he's brought?"

"I am. I came here with your guard's permission to learn the dimensions of the room in which we will perform. May I enter the room?"

The Lord and Lady smiled at her. The tall woman looked her over with stern, evaluative eyes. Nelleke hoped the woman did not identify her as one of the "accursed drinkers of human blood" she had just ranted over.

"If I am intruding, I will return to our place of

rehearsal, my Lord."

"You don't need to do that," William Percy said, giving the tall woman an admonishing look. "Please do your evaluation. And convey my greetings to Master Shakespeare, whom I look forward to meeting."

Nelleke bowed. The Percies and the tall woman left. Nelleke went back into the room. After waiting fifteen minutes just to be safe, she exited and went back to where she had seen Shakespeare, the King's Men, Anita, and Giles.

She stepped quietly into the room. The actors stood on stage and recited their lines. Anita stood off to the side near Shakespeare, who watched the rehearsal, arms crossed over his chest, his gaze intense. After a moment, Anita turned, did a double-take, and recognized Nelleke. Her eyes grew round with amazement. She hurried over to where Nelleke waited.

"Mother," she whispered. Nelleke smiled. Love and anxiety mixed in Anita's eyes. Glad to see her mother, she wondered what she was doing here and knew the danger she would face at a large estate where she might not be able to conceal herself during the day.

"I'm here on particular business."

Anita nodded. "Particular business" was the phrase Nelleke had always used to refer to matters related to her vampirism. "Are you busy? Can we talk?"

"I have to rehearse my part. Can you wait on me?"

"Of course," she answered, surprised that her daughter would play a part on stage. "Just note: I've told the people in the house that I'm part of the acting troupe. I'm not supposed to be here. So if anyone asks you, you know what to say."

"Yes, mother. I'll mention to the others that you came here to see me on a vital matter and have to maintain that you're a part of the troupe. They'll go along with it."

"Good. Are the children here?"

"Upstairs with a nurse."

Nelleke gave Anita a quick kiss and slipped back into the shadows. Both Shakespeare and the actors had been too absorbed in the rehearsal to notice her.

She walked a few steps, turned, and saw herself face to face with the tall woman. She cast a severe look at Nelleke. Nelleke bowed.

"What are you doing here?"

"We're rehearsing, my Lady. I stepped out for a moment to remember my lines."

"I don't know why, but I think you're lying. You're hiding something."

Nelleke did not reply. She tried to look astonished.

"Where are you from?"

"London."

"What is your name?"

"Nelleke Reitsma, and it please you."

"That isn't an English name. You have an accent."

"I come from the Low Countries. My English is not perfect."

The woman looked her over, snorted, turned, and hurried off. Nelleke hesitated and then followed her. Keeping a good distance, she trailed the woman. Expecting she would go to the parts of the house where the nobility lived, and puzzled no servant escorted her, Nelleke kept distance. The woman surprised her by going through a back door and out into the night.

She walked rapidly, her long white dress showing against the encroaching dark. Nelleke wondered how she made her way without a lantern but then saw that smooth white stones paved the path they walked along. She transformed to a bat and followed the woman's scent.

The woman continued on, walking probably two miles. Nelleke fluttered in the sky above her, swooping silently in wide loops, keeping her within the ken of her scent and sound.

She sensed the woman slowing down, lit in some bushes, and changed back to her human form.

Nelleke watched her quarry. She walked several steps, stopped, knelt, and raised her hands over her head. She uttered some sort of prayer or incantation in an odd-sounding language, rose, and stole into a thick wood of ancient gnarled trees. Nelleke followed.

The thicket blotted out stars and moon. The path of white stones had disappeared and in its place a dirt path traced through the wood. The woman seemed to know her way without looking. After ten minutes of rapid walking, she slowed. A white shape glowed ahead of them. The woman walked on, stopped, looked back, and parted a curtain of vines. The glow broke through the murk of the wood for a moment. Darkness and silence returned as the vines fell back into place.

Nelleke waited, listening. Unable to hear anything, she pushed through the covering of creepers and tendrils.

In front of her, a round structure that looked like an ancient Greek temple glowed in the light of the moon. Circular, with columns, it joined to a square building with a low, pointed roof. The stones of the place seemed to absorb and send back moonlight just as the path she had walked on earlier did. Nelleke stared.

A sharp, sudden pain tore through her body.

She dropped to her knees in agony. The right side of her upper body felt numb and on fire at the same time. The woman had thrown a knife or some other weapon pierced the right side of Nelleke's body just in the shoulder below her collarbone. As pain washed over her, she wondered why the vampire instincts that sensed and responded to danger had not taken over and made her skin hard so a weapon could not pierce it. Even if she had not seen the woman throw the missile at her, the supernatural perception that kept her from harm should have taken over; it always had before. But this time she had been hurt.

She grasped for the object with her free hand. She had not been hurt with a knife or small javelin. What her hand rested on an icicle. Waves of debilitating pain radiated from the wound. The right side of her body felt cold and useless.

"So," the woman said, stepping out of shadows. "My intuition proved true, praise be to Argruna. You're one of those blood-sucking, murderous vermin. I thought we'd killed all of you in these parts of our nation."

Nelleke felt her consciousness fading. Vampires were called the "undying," but they could be destroyed—by the sun, by a stake in that heart, or by magical spells. The woman came closer and spat on her.

"Whore," she hissed. "Twisted pervert. Why the Supreme Lord lets your type crawl on the face of this wholesome world I do not know." She extended her hand. From it, a long stiletto of ice flew out. It struck and embedded in Nelleke's left thigh. She screamed and fell flat, rolling on her back.

"This will not be an easy or pleasant way for you to die, you whore of the Devil," the woman hissed. "For me, though, it will be sheer pleasure to watch. You'll feel the terror of those you victimize and the pain of your prey. You will feel the abjection of the warrior-maiden Ayleth when one of your kind ripped her throat open and drank her life. You will feel the anguish of the goddess when she lost her belovéd. You pig. Human refuse. Scum of creation." She stood over her, her eyes filled with the fire of triumph, taking pleasure in the sight of Nelleke's pain and helplessness. She released another bolt of ice that struck her in the stomach.

"Die," she hissed. "Your vampire magic will not save you this time."

Nelleke felt the cold spreading through her body. Her ears began to ring. The excruciating pain she felt made her convulse violently. She wanted to scream for help but did not have enough breath in her lungs to do so. Head spinning, she looked up and saw the woman extend her hand to release another bolt of ice. Before she could, though, her body jerked violently. She fell to the ground. Nelleke saw Devyn standing behind her. He rushed over and crouched down.

Nelleke began to sob. The sharp swords of ice had torn her flesh violently and pierced her stomach. When danger called up her vampire spirit, her skin sealed and became impervious, able to repel musket balls and break steel blades, but for some reason, the ice shards had pierced through her flesh. She screamed as Devyn pulled the shard from her shoulder.

Her left side felt warm again. She cried out in pain as he wrenched the ice shard from her thigh and stomach. But the pain had begun to fade.

"Magic," he said. "But it didn't seem to protect her from a good knock on the head. I need to take this woman back to the cottage and secure her. She is a danger to us. I'm going to leave you here, Nelleke. I'll return or send someone to help you back. You'll start to recover soon, though. Will you trust me?" She nodded. He bent down and kissed her. "When you're able to get up, go hide in the woods. There may be others in the temple who can use magic against you."

"I'll wait," she answered, now able to speak.

Devyn turned, picked up the body of the woman, and hurried off into the dark.

Nelleke lay on the ground. She probed the wound on her shoulder. The place where the ice spike had gone in was closed up now. It no longer felt numb. She felt her thigh and abdomen begin to heal, sensing the internal bleeding she had felt stanch and her inner body repair itself. The bodies of vampires could become impervious, but when one of the undead was injured in some way, the same qualities that protected their bodies rapidly manifested to heal them. She lay on the ground, looking up at the trees and the stars and moon. Healing coursed through her. The magic—her magic, not the priestess's magic—had begun to work. In a few moments, she would be completely healed.

The woman, whoever she is, knows ancient of magic. She remembered the woman's evocation of the goddess Argruna. She remembered what Githa had said. The Percy family was more heretical than the authorities had imagined. Not only did they give allegiance to Roman Catholicism; they also worshiped an ancient goddess. They maintained a temple for the worship of Argruna. They kept a priestess, too. Their priestess knew sorcery that went back to the dawn of time. She had heard Clarice and Bernard speak of it in hushed tones. Vampires, even if they were ancient and powerful, feared what they called "ancient magic." She wondered how this woman knew such magic. She thought, as she felt her strength return, it might be ancient magic—magic and power the woman had attained through the worship of an ancient deity—magic from the dawn of time. She remembered what the woman had said in the library—worship for six-hundred years and one-hundred and fifty-one consecrated priestesses buried in the wood. If the succession of priestess went that far back in time, they might have access to the kind of sorcery vampires feared—the magic that had almost destroyed the northern covens and that, perhaps, she had felt in her encounter with the charm Githa had called the Emerald of Argruna.

Nelleke managed to get to her feet. Her wounds had healed. Her body felt warm again, though the woman's attack had left her weak. She stood, feeling her strength renew strongly, waiting until she had completely recovered.

She looked over at the building—it had to be a temple—glowing in the moonlight, silent and dark as a tomb. She heard crickets and peeper frogs. Quiet wind rustled the carpet of fallen leaves that never seemed to break down in old forests. Her heart filled with alarm when two figures stepped out of the tree line near the hedge, but the fear faded when she saw Desford and Clarice from the Coven of London. Clarice put her arms around Nelleke.

"Are you all right, child?"

"I've healed. Is all well? Did you secure that horrible woman who tried to kill me?"

"We've secured her. Samuel is there. His magic is greater than hers."

Nelleke had heard talk of Samuel. An ancient vampire who had lived from the days of King Alfred the Great, he practiced magic and was respected and feared even by ancient souls like Devyn and Clarice.

"We've questioned her. Devyn sent us to see what is inside the temple."

"It may be protected by an incantation, or there may be another priestess inside who possesses magic," Nelleke said, her voice taut with fear.

"Her magic is gone. She's being tortured now for information on what happened tonight. Samuel absorbed her magic and lifted the spells she had conjured to guard the Temple."

"She's being tortured?" Nelleke asked.

"It's the only we she'll tell us anything. We were ordered by Devyn to look inside. No harm awaits, but if you want to stay out here, you may."

Nelleke hesitated and then said, "I'll go with you."

The three of them made their way into the temple.

The circular formation at the front surrounded an image of the goddess Argruna. The marble from which it was sculpted was not white or black, but pink. In the smooth lines of the depiction, the goddess wore a flowing robe, had short, wavy hair, a stern face, and held a long, cruel-looking knife in her right hand (the knife, made of metal, silver, rested in a circle of the figure's sculpted fingers and caught a wisp in moonlight in its brightly polished blade).

Argruna's left hand was extended, palm up. In the palm, its shimmering green in sharp contrast to the pink stone of the sculpture, an emerald lay. For a long moment, the three of them gazed, held by the beauty and power of the statue.

"Let's see what's inside the other part of the Temple," Clarice said.

Going around the pink-stone image of deity, the three of them made their way into the interior, the holy place of the temple proper.

They went through a tiny anteroom with marble seats and kneeling benches. Once past this, Nelleke smelled the scent of living human bodies. In the dark, she saw two girls—one thirteen or so, the other no older than ten—lying in a bed, arms around each other, hair loose, lost in innocent sleep. *Acolytes*, she thought. *Girls in training to be priestesses.* One seemed to sense the presence of the intruders and stirred.

Clarice put a finger to her lips and nodded toward the door. The three of them stepped into the rotunda where the image of the goddess stood. Desford smiled triumphantly.

"So they maintain a heathen shrine—a shrine to the goddess Argruna. Our work will be quite easy. We just need to alert the local magistrate. The woman and her two little priestesses-in-training will go to the stake."

Clarice looked through the entrance at the sleeping girls.

"Have you ever seen anyone burned at the stake, Desford?"

He blinked at her. "No."

"You only recently crossed over. In my early days, it was a common punishment. I've seen it too many times, from the days of Wycliffe to the reign of Bloody Mary. It's more horrible than you can imagine." She looked down at the girls. "These two innocent girls dying in an ugly, prolonged agony—I don't want to see it or even contemplate it. We'll think of something to do with them."

"We could"—Desford gestured. Nelleke shuddered at

the thought of feeding on them.

"I will not allow that to happen," Clarice said "We'll leave them here for now. Let's go back to the house."

"Did you say Samuel is there?" Nelleke asked.

"He came from Calais when he heard what had happened."

"How did he get here from Calais?"

"He can be wherever he needs to be in an instant," Clarice told her. "He is not bound by distance. Besides the powers we all have, he has spent his whole life being an adept at magic. He is the only one of our people who knows the ancient magic." She seemed uncomfortable even speaking of Samuel. Nelleke did not know the name except from stories in the Bible. "At any rate," she continued, "Devyn is safe. Tristana is there and said the priestess's magic is insubstantial—weak and ineffective against the kind of magic Samuel and Tristana know. The woman has learned a few things that Samuel says any half-penny magician can learn but nothing of substance or power."

Nelleke shuddered. The woman's magic certainly had seemed formidable to her.

"She's no threat to us. Let's return to the cottage. Are you well enough to walk, Nelleke?"

"I've healed."

"We'll decide what course of action to take with these girls. They're only children. They need not be harmed. Come."

They made their way to the safe house. Nelleke told Clarice what the priestess had said to her in their encounter. As the three of them approached they heard prolonged screaming—a woman's voice. Nelleke recognized the voice as belonging to the priestess.

Once inside, they found Devyn and Tristana. Another figure Nelleke did not know but assumed must be Samuel stood beside Devyn. They were speaking Latin, though their conversation went too fast for her to catch much of it. She stepped over to see what had absorbed their attention and was shocked by what she saw.

They had stripped the priestess naked and tied her to a chair. Nelleke saw what looked like metal cones attached to her hands and realized after a moment they were thumbscrews. An expression of agony distorted her face. Her mouth hung open. She gasped for air. Her eyes were frantic with pain. "Mercy," she gasped, barely able to speak. "Mercy! For the love of the goddess!"

"Tell us what we want to know and we'll release you."

The woman only wept. Clarice stepped forward.

"Listen to me, woman. We have found the two girls you have in your temple. We don't want to harm them. Do I need to say more?"

Her face drawn with agony, she nodded and then said, "I'll tell you everything. Please, for the love of mercy!"

Devyn released the mechanisms on the torture devices and released the ropes they had used to hold her hands in place. The moment, he took them off the woman sobbed loudly began to suck her thumbs.

"Cover her nakedness," Clarice ordered. Tristana threw the same blanket Devyn had given Nelleke to wrap up in over the priestess's shoulders. She sobbed and trembled. Samuel touched her hands. Her face registered amazement as the pain she felt ceased. She stared up at him in fear. Clarice stepped around to face her.

"I am Clarice. I am the leader of this group. Tell me your name."

"My name is sacred to the goddess," she said. "I am not allowed to reveal it to anyone outside our community."

"If you don't want us to put the devices on your hands again, answer. Not everyone here is convinced that you should be treated with compassion—you or your acolytes may come to harm if you persist in this line of reply. I think it will be better if you tell us your name."

She looked up with weary eyes. "I am Emeline."

"Emeline, you know we have the jewel. Nelleke—the woman you tried to kill—said she heard you say it is the embodiment of the goddess Argruna, to whom you have given your life in service. We can destroy the stone. We can shatter it with a hammer. We can embed it in mortar and drop it in the depths of sea, silencing her forever."

"You have won and I yield. The goddess will be no more. I and Jacquelyn and Maerwynn—the young maidens who are training to be priestess but now will never attain that—will pour out our blood as a final sacrifice to her name."

"Do you have to do that?"

"Yes," she said, her voice hard. "We are dedicated, body and soul, to Argruna. If she ceases to be, we have no reason to live."

"I know the story of the warrior maiden one of our kind killed. I know her death is the reason Argruna hates us. What was the girl's name?"

"Ayleth."

"A lovely name. Don't you think the vampire who killed her did not know he was offending the goddess? He was only satisfying necessity."

"She was killed by a woman, not a man. But none of these things matter now. I know you're going to kill me. I only ask that you will allow me to die in the purity in which I have lived. And the girls—it is proper they follow me in death. They are only children, but they are holy to the goddess. All is lost to us."

"What happened was unfortunate, though whoever took the young woman's life did so out of nothing other than the urge to preserve her own life. I can understand how Argruna would be angered by the loss of her belovéd. But it was not from malice or spite. Surely the goddess would understand as much."

"I cannot speak for the goddess and would never dare to speak for her. I do not control her heart. I am her servant, not her mistress. I only know my duty. I must obey. My acolytes"—

"I can't let allow you harm those two little girls. We will care for them," Clarice said, her voice firm. "We will find someone to raise them and will not harm them in any way. As for you, Emeline, I would think the goddess would have you live. You've served her faithfully. The things that happened did not happen because of you."

Emeline only shook her head.

"Very well. You are free to go. Promise me, in the name of the goddess, you will not try to abduct those two young maidens and harm them."

"You have my word as the last priestess of Argruna."

Nelleke took her into the bedroom and helped her dress. Emeline emerged, looked at the room full of vampires, turned, and wearily walked out into the night. Clarice turned to Tristana.

"Transform and fly to the temple. Make certain she does not harm those maidens."

Tristana nodded and hurried out the door.

Clarice turned to the others. "We need to finish our mission here," she said. "Samuel, will you care for the emerald that carries the spirit of the goddess, and the book of moon runes as well?"

"I will, my lady."

Clarice turned to the other. "Then let's go."

That very night the vampires sent word to the Privy Council's agents, who were staying nearby. Devyn and the others entered the manse by stealth. He and Nelleke made their way to the library. Lurking in the shadows, they waited until the priest hiding there appeared. He pulled open a door hidden beneath the table. Devyn stepped out of the shadows and hypnotized him. He collapsed on the stairs that led down into his hiding place.

Things fell out in short order. The Privy Council agents arrived, arrested the priest and confiscated the books and pamphlets they found in his hiding place. A search of the estate uncovered a chapel where illegal worship took place. Devyn led them to the pagan Temple, though he suggested it was simply one of the oddities that had sprung up around the country of late that celebrated Greek and Roman learning. He and Samuel had taken the image of Argruna out of the anteroom and stored in the safe house, wanting to preserve it both as a prize of war and for its beauty and charm. Eventually it would end up in the British Museum. One of Nelleke's album covers featured her standing in front of it.

A week later, some five miles from the house, they found the body of a woman who had apparently cut her own throat. No one in the area seemed to know her. After inquiries yielded no information, the authorities buried her in a potter's field in an unmarked grave.

The Percies were arrested and shipped off to the Tower to await trial. Lord Cecil's agents said the Crown would confiscated their monies and properties. He gave a substantial reward to the servant girl Kaylein for her help. She eventually moved to London, married, and lived a long happy life there. The next day, Lord Cecil arrived. He met with Devyn, Clarice, and Nelleke by night, thanked them, and asked if they thought Shakespeare and his troupe was in collusion with the Percies.

"There is some evidence of Papist influence in his life," Devyn said. "The man studied under several schoolmasters with Catholic sympathies and, in his youth, boarded with a man of Roman leanings. His wife's family are determined Papists."

Devyn did not know Shakespeare, but Nelleke did.

"Let me speak with him," she said. "I'll simply ask him. He usually tells the truth."

The moon hung full in a sky of wild stars. Nelleke met with Shakespeare in the library. He looked shaken.

"Are you well, Master Shakespeare?" she asked.

"I'm a little nervous, to tell you the truth. I think you remember what we talked about before. There are some connections in my past I would rather not be uncovered."

"They already know about them. Lord Cecil wonders if you're a Papist. He says your father was fined for not going to church."

Shakespeare smiled. "That's only because he knew he would be arrested for debt the moment he left his own home for a public place." He seemed to want to say more but stopped.

"Go on, William. You can tell me. You know I'll be discreet."

"Quite frankly," Shakespeare said, "I'm skeptical about the whole thing. Undoubtedly, something is out there, but I think we should be humble before the divine, not militant. All the damning, arresting, torturing, and murdering over who has properly or improperly interpreted the scriptures nauseates me. I go to the church the King endorses and follow its decrees and its beliefs. Wherever my heart may wander—well, I have no control over that."

"I wouldn't go about saying such things—though I'm in complete agreement with you. I'll tell Cecil you're loyal to our church. He gives heed to my counsel."

"And how did this come about?"

"Perhaps someday I'll tell you. But not yet."

"Too bad Anita won't get to play on stage."

"Ah, but she will. Cecil has brought in a Percy family member who is a loyal Protestant and has installed him as manager here until Cecil determines what will become of the estate. The relative and his family and staff are coming here tonight. There are to be ceremonies. Perhaps the play can be staged as a part of the festivities for his installation."

Nelleke smiled. "Wonderful. I told a number of people here I was an actress. That was subterfuge, of course, but I wonder if I might participate."

"Well," he said, an apologetic look on his face, "we have your child Anita playing Phryinia, who is a prostitute. The script calls for two prostitutes, but we combined the roles into one. Would you be willing to play a whore?"

"I would do quite well in such a role—I'd only have to act my nature."

Shakespeare did not know what to say.

XV

The performance went off as scheduled. Some of the audience members complained that Shakespeare had put women on stage.

"They're whores, too," one woman exclaimed. "It's scandalous!"

Someone told her the French allowed women to act on stage, and that the women weren't whores, they were only acting the part of whores.

Nelleke and Anita worked on their lines. That night they performed. Their part was small, but their provocative dress and bawdy mannerisms got laughs, whistles, and shouted comments from the audience. When Timon of Athens (played by Giles) revealed that he had found a buried treasure with enough gold "to make a whore foreswear her trade," the audience roared with laughter because Nelleke and Anita had characterized those who ply the trade so well. When the two of them held up their skirts to catch the coins Timon threw their way (uncovering their knickers, garters, and hose) peals of bawdy laughter and applause followed. They were only on stage ten minutes, exited, changed out of their costumes, found a place in the back row, and watched the remainder of the production.

"This play is one of his philosophical plays," Anita said. "I think he co-authored it. It's a bit boring."

"I liked it."

"You would, Mother. If women were allowed to be philosophers, I think you would rank with them, like Hypatia of Alexandria." She paused and said, "Thank you for standing as our advocate. Don't say you didn't. I know you did. Master Shakespeare has long been under suspicion because his father's family harbored improper religious convictions. Really, he doesn't care a fig about religion. I guess that's just as bad as being a Papist. And you, Mother, should visit us more often."

"I've been busy, but I will, child."

"Though, of course, people will wonder why you look as young as I look. I imagine William does."

Nelleke said she was sure he noticed it.

A few days later, she arrived back in London. A letter from Carmilla awaited her. She had settled and had a secure place in German territory. Nelleke resolved to write back. If she ever travelled that way, she would visit.

Devyn had suggested she serve on the Council.

"I'm a child," she said—*child* being a term the undead used for one who has not lived long as a vampire.

"Children sometimes have discernment to which adults never attain. Doesn't the Bible say, 'Out of the mouths of babes and sucklings cometh wisdom'?"

Nelleke remembered studying the Bible with the nuns in her home town. "It doesn't say that exactly, but you're close."

"Think about it, Nelleke."

Later that day, Tristana visited. They drank tea and ate scones.

"I'm going to care for those two little girls," Tristana said.

"I thought Clarice planned to have one of her mortal friends to adopt them."

"She wanted to, but I want to raise them."

"Why might that be?"

"I had children, like you had a child. Like you, I raised them after I crossed over. They were both boys."

"You never told me that."

"It's difficult to talk about. I married at sixteen and bore two children in the first two years of my marriage. The second birth almost killed me and I could not get pregnant again after that. When my boys were five and six, I crossed over. I desperately wanted my boys, so I took them by night. The first year I fled to various places until I met Bernard and he helped me arrange things so I could raise them. Once I met up with the London coven, it got better. I had help and support. Like Anita, the boys knew about my being one of the undying. They grew up into fine men. They're both gone now. One of the pains of living forever is that you see mortals you love die."

"Yes. I'll see that myself someday."

"There's another reason, too," Tristana said.

Seeing the look on her face, Nelleke lowered her voice.

"Do you wish to speak of it?"

"I don't, but I need to. Nelleke, I was the one who killed Ayleth."

Silence fell. Nelleke wanted to say something but decided this was not the right time to speak. Tristana continued.

"I had seen her in the woods often. She was a woman of the woods and a shield maid. Had I known she was the belovéd of a deity, I would not have preyed upon her."

Silence came. After a long pause, Nelleke spoke.

"Devyn told me what had been a mystery for hundreds of years: that it was Argruna who killed so many of our people in the Northern provinces. She was looking for me. When she couldn't find me, she apparently gave up and transformed herself to a jewel because she couldn't bear living in grief and frustration."

After a long silence, Nelleke said, "I'm sorry, Tristana."

She shrugged. "I guess it wasn't really my fault, though now that I know I blame myself for it—and for the deaths of so many of our brothers and sisters in the north. Can I bring the girls over some time, Nelleke? Will you teach them to play the lute?" Her eyes glistened with tears. "I want them to know beauty and goodness and music. I'll let them go someday, but now it seems like I have my own children back." She smiled a sad smile. "I never had girls."

"They're a blessing," Nelleke said, putting her arms around Tristana. "And, yes, of course I'll teach them. You look tired. Why don't you lie down? You look like you could use some rest."

Tristana brought the two girls over the next night. Nelleke taught them how to hold, tune, and strum her lute. Before dawn came, they left.

The house grew quiet. Nelleke did not feel sleepy. She sat in her bedroom, the thick, black curtains on the windows keeping out destructive sunlight. She wondered what the future would hold. She wondered if Izaak would return. She wondered if Devyn felt any true affection for her. She wondered about the future.

She kept her eyes fixed on the lute hanging from a hook beside her bed.

XIV

Nelleke finished her concert at Carnegie Hall, and stood to take a bow. The same lute she held in her hands had hung on the wall of that old bedroom in London where passion had transpired and dreams frightened or delighted her. Pages of the suite John Bull had written for her had lain on the table by her bed—only they were not a printed copy back then but a copy written in his own hand. When the applause died down at the bright concert venue, she blew a kiss to the crowd and walked off stage. They kept applauding, cheering, and whistling. She would give them an encore, of course. She would play a short piece that a composer in London, Pierson Matthews, had written for her. She always presented it as an English folksong and claimed to have found it in the archives of the old library where she had found the John Bull composition. Though she and Pierson had been lovers only a short while and he had gone to the north and eventually married a vampire woman named Deoch, she still remembered him with fondness. He and Deoch presently lived with Githa in Carlyle, Scotland. After playing the piece, she would find refuge in the hotel room she had rented. Maybe she would call Izaak. He was in the States, though not in New York. Maybe he would come to see her.

She walked out on stage to play the encore that would end her concert for that night.

About the Author

David W. Landrum lives and writes in West Michigan. His fiction, poetry, and scholarships have appeared in journals and magazines around the world.

Landrum has published over 150 short stories in such journals as The Horror Zine, 34th Parallel, Black Denim Review, Silver Pen, Erotique, Non-Binary Review, Night to Dawn, The Lorelei Signal and in many others. His novellas—The Gallery, Strange Brew, ShadowCity, The Last Minstrel, Le Café de la Mort, Mother Hulda, The Prophetess, and The Sorceress of Time, along with his full-length fantasy novel, The Sorceress of the Northern Seas, are available through Amazon. He has also published a great deal of poetry and many academic studies.

You can find more about David W. Landrum's writing at the following sites:

http://davelandrum.wix.com/davidwlandrum

https://www.facebook.com/David-W-Landrum-956574837687425/

http://www.amazon.com/David-W.-Landrum/e/B00HBXGI64/ref=sr_tc_2_0?qid=1457454518&sr=1-2-ent

http://davidwlandrum.blogspot.com/

Excerpt from
SINFONIA II:
A PAINTED LADY

"Where is he?" Nelleke asked.

"Ephraim's Hill," Julian answered.

"I'll lock up and we'll go after him."

Nelleke secured the house; both of them transformed to bats and rose up in the warm summer air.

They flew over the town of Sinfonia, population around 20,000, located in the delta land of the White River in northern Arkansas. Though deprived of sight in the form they had taken, the two of them could sense the town and identify Cynthia's car as she drove through the four stoplights on the city's main street and, though she did not know it, toward the place where her ex-husband lay in wait to kill her. Through the sounds they emitted, they knew they had passed over the city. They flew quickly—quickly enough to beat Cynthia to Ephraim's Hill.

They set down in a newly plowed field, transforming back to their human selves. Their senses had sharpened by now. Their bodies had transformed to manifest the features both exhibited when in danger or when they hunted. Perception heightened, they immediately caught Cynthia's abusive ex-husband's scent.

"He has a shotgun," Izaak said. Nelleke could smell the gun oil and powder.

"So the bastard really is planning to kill her."

"I told you he was."

They made their way across the field and into the tree line near a bend in the road. It was a good place to lie in ambush for someone driving a car: a sharp curve in the road required that one slow down considerably to negotiate it. He would have had plenty of time to get a shot at her from his hiding place behind a large rock. Not tonight, Nelleke thought, and not ever again after tonight.

He did not sense them until they were right on him. Nelleke cleared her throat. The man turned, pointing the shotgun.

"Who the hell are you and what are you doing here?"

"We came to stop you from killing Cynthia."

He said nothing, but Nelleke saw him tense and raise the barrel of the shotgun so it would hit their faces if he fired.

"Are you cops?"

"No, we're vampires," Izaak said.

He made a sound somewhere between a laughing and spitting. "If I were you, I wouldn't be telling stupid jokes at a time like this. You're playing a dangerous game." He licked his lips. "In fact, you've given me no choice. I'm going to take both of you out."

Nelleke and Izaak said nothing. They faced him in the quiet, warm dark.

"You think I'm fucking with you? I am not fucking with you."

"Did you get that line from Glengarry Glen Ross?" Izaak asked. Nelleke laughed.

He didn't know what they meant and or why the girl seemed to think what the man with her said was so funny. After a moment's pause, he discharged the shotgun at Izaak, quickly pumped another shell into the chamber and shot Nelleke.

When they smoke cleared, they stood facing him, both of them unscathed. The pellets had torn their clothing but done nothing to damage their physical bodies. Cynthia's ex-husband stared at them. Before he could move, Nelleke lunged, swung her arm, and connected with the side of his head with a crunch. Neck broken, he crumpled to the ground.

The two of them shared his blood, taking turns sucking it from the gaping wound Izaak scored on the right side of his neck. When they had sucked him dry, they carried his body to a swampy area near Salado Creek and left him by the bank. The supernatural creatures who carried off the bodies of those they killed would find him. Other than a little of his blood that had trickled on the ground, there would be no trace of him. Moonlight glittered on the water as they turned to go. The police would discover the man's car and his abandoned shotgun. They might find some of his blood. His disappearance would be a matter of public notice for maybe a year and then he would be forgotten—forgotten, Nelleke hoped, by Cynthia as well. She smiled in satisfaction.

They transformed and flew three miles to the small house Izaak owned. Once inside, he got out a shirt and the blouse Nelleke had given him yesterday to store there. Just after she removed the purple top shredded by shotgun fire, he cupped his hands under her breasts.

"It turns me on when you wear a black bra," he said.

She laughed. "It turned you on when I wore a linen bra back in the 1600s and the corset push-up bra I wore in the Victorian era."

"It's all about what lies beneath," he said, kissing her and adroitly undoing the snap. She held her arms straight so the bra slipped off and kicked it away. Izaak kissed Nelleke. Drinking blood always got her going, he knew, and he had been away in New York and Indianapolis and had missed her. Kissing her, squeezing her breasts—so white in the moonlight filtering through the windows—he felt her respond.

"You bought a bigger bed, didn't you?" she asked

dreamily.

"No—but we'll make do."

"I hate that bed. I don't see how you sleep on it. No way am I going to let you fuck me there. Let's go outside."

They walked out the back door. Creatures of all sorts abounded around Izaak's place, but animals could sense vampires and gave them a wide berth. Behind the woodshed fifty feet from the house, they slipped into a grassy enclave surrounded by pine trees. A raccoon scurried out when they came into the clearing. Nelleke had brought along the damaged blouse and spread it on the grass. Izaak would know—she remembered how many centuries they had been lovers—what she wanted and how she wanted it. Foreplay would annoy her. He took her in his arms at once.

As he made love to her it was all heat, longing, and passion. Her lust rose to its highest point after she had drunk blood. Desire ruled her. It ran with the starkness of a lightning streak on a dark night, flashing as often as Izaak thrust into her with an easy, deep rhythm. She writhed, bucked, and shouted; swore and cursed, even sang (she was, after all, a professional musician). Orgasms came like constellations in deep space, each one spectacular and unique, with its own shape, coloration, and contour. She felt him tense and empty his seed into her—fruitless seed; vampires could not produce children. Silence then. The sound of cicadas and crickets, the sound of water rushing over rocks in a small creek that ran behind the house arose as the two pulled and apart and love side by side.

As she lay there, she thought of how only an hour ago, she and Cynthia had been sitting in the living room of her home, Cynthia conducting an interview.

"I have to compliment you on the marvelous and beautiful way you've restored this house," Cynthia Blake, a journalist from Little Rock had told Nelleke. "It's such a pity it sat neglected for so many years—such a beautiful home and of significant historical value. I think everyone in the community is happy to see it returned to its past glory. And that leads me to the question with which I wanted to begin the interview. Why would someone as well-known and talented as Nelleke Reitsma chose to settle in Sinfonia, Arkansas?"

They sat in the ornate living room of the house Nelleke had restored to its past Victorian glory. She had named it the "Painted Lady," a term used to characterize a certain style of house, but Nelleke had thought it applied so well to her new residence she had also chosen it as a name for her place. She smiled. "Sinfonia is a lovely city. And I'm not certain I'm that well-known."

"Classical Guitar magazine rated you as one of the top ten women guitarists in the world; and the number one female lutenist."

"As far as the lute performance goes, it's because I'm about the only woman in the world who plays the lute. As for the other honor—well, I'm flattered."

"So why settle here?"

"Peace and quiet. I've never liked the noise and bustle of big cities. I grew up in a small town in Holland but moved to London when I was young and lived there quite a few years. I finally decided to move to a smaller place. A relative of mine owned land here that no one has lived in for years—and this house. So I had the house repaired and restored. I've lived here three months and love it. It's a good place to live, to practice, and to write music. I'm getting know the people here and look forward to being part of the community."

"Well, we're certainly glad to have you here."

"I'm happy to be here I'm looking forward to the years to come."

With that, the interview ended. Nelleke invited Cynthia to have a drink with her. Her filming crew began packing up their equipment. She asked for brandy. Nelleke poured two.

"I'm glad you could make it for the interview. I heard what happened."

Cynthia winced. "It's embarrassing to suddenly be in the news that way—especially when you're a journalist."

"If you don't want to talk about it, you needn't."

"He's been released on bond. Like a lot of relationships where this sort of thing happens, I was an enabler. I put up with his abuse for a lot of years. No more. I'm pressing charges on this last incident. I have witnesses. He's going in the slammer again—this time for good, I hope."

They switched to other topics. Nelleke talked about her career and about living in London. Cynthia recalled the interesting people she had interviewed in her career as journalist. The two women spent an hour enjoying brandy and conversation. After a while, Izaak came in. Nelleke introduced him a "friend." The hands on her mantle clock said it was near twelve.

"I need to go," Cynthia said. "It's a long drive back to Little Rock."

Nelleke and Izaak escorted her to his car. Stars blazed in the sky above. Out here you could see the Milky Way, Nelleke reflected, the old sky she remembered from her the days before light pollution dulled the heavens. Cynthia took leave of them and drove off. Then they had transformed and gone after her abusive spouse.

Nelleke let her mind return to the bed, its warmth, and the marvelous satisfaction she felt. She snuggled closer to Izaak. "What did you find out when you were in Indy?" she asked.

"Clarice is coming here."

Nelleke pushed herself up on one elbow.

"What does Clarice want?"

"She didn't say."

"When is she getting here?"

"She'll be here on Tuesday. She's planning to stay with you—at the Painted Lady."

"That's a hell of a note." Actually, Nelleke liked Clarice and respected her wisdom. But why would she be coming to the United States? Nelleke had settled in that country to decrease the possibility of people recognizing her. She had lived almost 300 years in England. And in the sixties, she achieved a degree of celebrity as a musician and music producer. Once again, in the new millennium, she had come into the limelight. This was probably what Clarice wanted to talk to her about.

"I hope I'm not in trouble."

"Me too. But we've been good little vampires. I don't see how we could have gotten on the coven's bad side."

They got up, washed, and got dressed.

Nelleke had given Izaak a ride to her place and he had left his car at his house as part of the plan to kill Cynthia's ex-husband. They climbed in Izaak's Impala and drove back to Sinfonia. Just after they arrived, her cellphone rang—it was Clarice, who said she would be there the day after tomorrow.